BOOKS BY PATRICIA McKILLIP

The Throme of the Erril of Sherill
The House on Parchment Street
The Forgotten Beasts of Eld
The Night Gift
The Riddle-Master of Hed
Heir of Sea and Fire
Harpist in the Wind
Stepping From the Shadows
Moon-Flash

MOON-FLASH

MOON-FLASH

by Patricia A. McKillip

An Argo Book

ATHENEUM · NEW YORK

1984

To

my father,

whatever dream

he's in

Library of Congress Cataloging in Publication Data

McKillip, Patricia A.
Moon-flash.

"An Argo book."
[1. Fantasy]   I. Title.
PZ7.M19864Mo   1984   [Fic]   84–2974
ISBN 0–689–31049–8

Published simultaneously in Canada by
McClelland & Stewart, Ltd.
Composition by Maryland Linotype,
Baltimore, Maryland
Printed and bound by Fairfield Graphics,
Fairfield, Pennsylvania
Designed by Mary Ahern
First Edition

MOON-FLASH

1

KYREOL'S EYES were so dark that if she looked at you between leaves you couldn't see them. Her skin was the color of a shadow, and her hair was blacker than that. She was tall for her age, and lean, a great tree-climber and a magnificent storyteller. She knew all the secret places in the world—the bramble-cave in the forest, the pool beneath the falls where the great fish sunned, the hollow tree—for she had walked from the Beginning of world halfway to its End. The world began at the Face and ended at Fourteen Falls; it was bounded by forests, and the River ran through the center of it, giving life and carrying it away. Kyreol had fished in the River, sailed on it, swam in it, thrown rocks and flowers at it, learned stories from it, and watched herself grow in its reflection year by year. On the day she became a woman, she gazed into the water, searching for signs of the change on her face, and remembered that she had been betrothed since the day she was born.

Kyreol's mother had betrothed her to Tarvar's youngest son, Korre. He lived downriver, at Turtle-

Crossing, and Kyreol knew him only vaguely. He was a short, dark, serious boy with a shy smile. She saw him mostly from a distance in his boat, for he had a handful of sisters to fish for. Since Kyreol's mother had vanished off the face of the world ten Moon-Flashes before, Kyreol had to tell her father that she was ready for the betrothal ritual. Then, since she had no sisters, she had to make her own betrothal skirt. The ritual was to be held at Moon-Flash; and the next Moon-Flash, her father told her, was very soon. So Kyreol, who hated sewing, sat in the quiet of her house, an upside-down bowl of mud and dark river rock, surrounded by piles of green and red and gold feathers. She threaded them together slowly and told stories to herself for comfort.

"My mother went to Fourteen Falls and turned into a rainbow . . .

"She walked through the forest toward sunrise. She travelled from Flash to Flash across the world until—until . . ." Kyreol smiled. "She found a place-name. And the place-name was River-Tree. Her home. She walked all the way—" Her hands stilled. She gazed out a round window across the River as if she were watching her mother return from a walk of ten Flashes. She frowned suddenly. "Wait. If she went that way—" She pointed the hand with the needle in it behind her—"how could she come back this way?" She pointed the hand with the feather in it in front of her. It was in this position that Terje found her.

He dropped a bag of feathers at her feet, eyeing her unsurprisedly. He lived at Three Rocks, and he had been with Kyreol more often than not since they were tiny children. They had grown together; they had learned words from each other and fed each other berries. They spent nights on the riverbanks together talking about the world. Now Kyreol was going away from Terje to live with another family at Turtle-Crossing. Terje scowled at her. She stood up impetuously, scattering feathers, thinking only of her question.

"Terje, what shape is the world?"

He nudged a feather with his toe. "The River is the World. Is that all you've done? Two rows of feathers?"

"But what if I walked away from the River. Sideways across the world. Would I fall off? Maybe my mother fell off the end of the world?"

He stared at her. He was a little shorter than she. His skin and hair and eyes were the color of honey, and the muscles swam like fish over his bones. Something made his scowl deepen; his eyes fell away from her. "My mother sent these feathers," he said gruffly. "I'll help you."

"I am a woman now," she said with dignity. "I can sew my own skirt." She slid her bone needle through the shaft of a feather and poked herself in the thumb. She shook her hand and sucked it, while Terje laughed. He threaded three feathers neatly, then stopped and sighed.

"What about our boat? Yours and mine? We built it together."

"You keep it."

"What about the time you fell out of a tree and broke your wrist and I put mud and leaves around it for you?"

Her brows crinkled, as she finally sensed what he was trying to tell her. "Oh, Terje," she said softly.

"I didn't know it would be so soon. But we couldn't stay children forever. Anyway, you'll be betrothed soon, and some other girl will come and live with you at Three Rocks . . ." Her brows crept even closer as she said that. She tossed her long hair suddenly, making feathers whirl. "Anyway, let's not think about it."

"Will you miss me?"

"Well, Terje, this is the way the world is. It was all decided before you and I could talk. My mother decided." With a swift change of mood, she flung feathers angrily into the air. "And then she vanished. It wasn't fair; she didn't even stay to help me with this—"

"The River reached out and took her," Terje whispered.

"No." She was silent a long time. "My father said she left him. She went away. He said it once. Then he never spoke of her again."

"Away," Terje said bewilderedly. "Where is there to go? Past Fourteen Falls? Up the Face? The River is the world, and all the places in it are named."

Kyreol shrugged. "Maybe she flew to O. I don't know. She turned into a bird and—Terje, guess how the moon O got its name."

"How?"

She giggled. "The first person in the world looked up at it and said—"

"Oh."

"Terje, who was the first person in the world?"

"How would I know?" he demanded.

"Well, think." She paused. "First there was the River. With no names. No people. And then one day there were people. And they saw turtles coming out

6

of the River to lay their eggs, so they called that place Turtle-Crossing. And maybe they had a boat, and it snagged on the sand, so they call that place Sandspit. And they saw a tree with pink and green leaves as big as your face and called it—No. The tree would have been a baby, then. Maybe it wouldn't even have— maybe there were no trees. So long ago. Where did they come from? The first people?"

Terje drew a deep breath and closed his mouth. "I think," he said glumly, "you will sew this skirt and get betrothed, and then marry and have babies, and you'll tell them your stories and not me. So what does it matter where the first people came from?"

Kyreol sewed in silence for a while. Then the grave look left her face and she smiled again. "The River-Tree bore them. Inside its pods. They dropped to the ground and cracked, and the First People came out. Little, tiny people. A man and a woman . . ."

Kyreol's father found them later, sewing diligently in a colorful pool of feathers. He smelled of mist and cold stone, and Kyreol knew he had been upriver, near the Face. The Face was a solid black wall of rock, the boundary of the world. It rose so high that the moon rested behind it by day, and the sun by night. The River was born at the top, uncoiled itself, roared through the air, skimmed down and down the black precipice, to churn deep into the vast bowl it had carved at the bottom of the Face. Kyreol's father, who healed and explained dreams and bestowed the blessings of the River and the Moon-Flash on all their lives, sometimes went to the edge of the bowl to think. What he thought about there, he never told Kyreol.

Terje dropped his needle and scrambled to his feet.

Icrane was as dark as Kyreol. He wasn't a tall man, but he was broad and muscular. His still, flat face tended to look fierce, though he was gentle-natured. He gazed at Terje absently, probably, Kyreol thought, not even really seeing him. But the blood flushed into Terje's face, and he said, awkward for some reason,

"I was helping Kyreol sew."

Icrane nodded, unsurprised. He put his big hand on the back of Terje's head, in a gesture that was at once a caress and a nudge toward the door. "Your father is looking for you. And it is time for me to speak to Kyreol about the betrothal ceremony."

He sat down amidst the feathers, threaded them as he spoke. Kyreol tried to listen; her mind kept filling with pictures of his words. *Crowd, feast, birds, cave—*

"How long?" she interrupted.

"Until you dream. Then you mark the wall and leave."

Fire, Moon-Flash, betrothal. It seemed a dream itself that her father was saying these things to her. A cave behind the falls at the Face, a hundred red birds released at the Flash in her name. She wondered for the first time what her betrothed was doing, whether he had listened to the same words, if he were excited, too. Feeling old and dignified and strange to herself, she put her hand on Icrane's knee, stopping him.

"Where did my mother go?" Her voice sounded queer. "Did you ever dream where she went?"

For a moment Icrane was not going to answer her. His face grew empty and his eyes went flat, as when he was angry or offended. Then he seemed to remember that her mother had bound them together, he and

Kyreol. His face opened again; he looked down at the floor, frowning a little, no longer the Healer, her father, but a man who had been hurt long ago and was still puzzled by it.

"Once," he said. He cleared his throat. "I dreamed —I dreamed of a stone. A beautiful crystal. First the stone opened and said her name. Then I saw her holding the stone. Then it was in the sky, a star, and she was following it. I woke and knew she had not died in the River, she had gone away from me."

"Where?"

He shook his head. "The River is the world. She— maybe into a dream. I don't know. I didn't know I had made her unhappy."

"I wish I remembered her face."

Her father brushed her cheek with his palm. "She looked like you."

The world, Kyreol thought later, throwing stones into the wide River, stretches up to the Face and down to Fourteen Falls. People found places on it to live and named them. Three Rocks, Green Pool, Little Stream. . . *Our houses are built of trees and riverstone, the River and the forest feed us, we wear what the animals wear. But.* A stone plopped into the water; the water jumped upward, then spread itself into smooth, widening rings, rippling and breaking at her feet. Her thoughts veered. *Why are so many things round?* she wondered. *The moon is round, the water-circles are round, Terje's eyes are round, dark then light, rimmed with circles of dark. The stone I threw wasn't round, but the ripples it made were. . . Why? Where could my mother have gone? Past Fourteen Falls? Why?*

A twig snapped. She turned, thinking Terje was

looking for her, and slid easily, noiselessly into the shadowed crook of a tree. It was dusk. Tiny flying things hovered above the quiet River; fish leaped to feed on them, vanished back into the circles they had made. Wood smoke hazed the evening. The first tiny stars were appearing. Leaves rustled. *I am invisible,* she thought. *I am night, and this tree, I am smoke.* She waited, enjoying herself, thinking of Terje falling into the River in shock when she leaped out at him. *I am a bad night-spirit, a wicked dream* . . . But it wasn't Terje.

It was a man she didn't recognize. She stopped herself from jumping at him, then opened her mouth to greet him, then realized she didn't know his name. He walked oddly, very quietly, as though he were stalking someone else. A hunter, maybe, from downriver. But he had no bow or spear or knife. He was very tall; his face was half-hidden by his feather hood. What she could see of it was dark and proudly made. His feet were bare; he wore a band of dappled hawk feathers about one knee. A hunter. But he wasn't hunting. So why was he so silent? He stopped near her, and her breath stopped.

He shifted back his hood, watched the cold luminous moon beginning to rise above the Face. He stayed still so long that Kyreol's feet began to ache in the chilly water. She could have moved, greeted him, but she was too curious, and all the night-instincts were awake in her blood. He moved finally, when it was almost too dark for her to see.

He lifted his hand. Something glittered in it: a piece of O, a mingling of water and moonlight. He spoke to the glittering. So it was a talisman, a magic

part of his hunting, the place where he kept his good
fortune. But his words made no sense. "Nine point
three point four," he said very softly. "The Face."

He closed his hand over the gleam. Kyreol blinked.
For a moment she still saw him, a lean shadow etched
against darkness. Then a dry leaf crackled, and he
merged into the night.

She thought about him for a night and half a day,
then suddenly there was no more time for thinking.
There were women everywhere, cooking so much food
she thought no one would ever have to eat again. They
brought her gifts: a jacket of blue feathers, a gold
hood, ankle bracelets. They finished her feather skirt;
and at the dawn of Moon-Flash, they dyed her face,
painted her eyelids and mouth, drew fire and the
moon on her forehead, the River, and the River-Tree,
so that the moon would know where she lived. When
she looked at her reflection in the water, she knew
that her old life had stopped, gone away, and nothing
would ever bring it back. She thought of Terje and
knew that he was gone, too, with all of her past, and
her throat burned. But the stranger's face looking back
at her had no past, only a future, and Kyreol could
not cry her tears. Then the sun rose and she was being
carried on a skin stretched taut by the family of her
betrothed, upriver toward the Face.

The journey took half a day. People kept joining
them, vividly clothed and painted, laughing, chattering, carrying food, wine made of fermented honey and
nuts, and cages of bright red birds. Kyreol sat silently,
too unused to her new self to talk. Her father, leading
the procession, was also silent. They reached the Face
at noon. The River-people spread their feast on a

clearing away from the spray and thunder of the Falls and sat down to wait. Kyreol followed her father alone to the dream-cave.

The spray was blinding. It rolled off the feathers covering her, but her face and hands turned icy. She didn't dare brush the water off her face lest she wash off her tree-sign and the moon no longer recognize her. She wished she could take her father's hand, going up the steep, wet trail, but she was no longer a child. Neither of them spoke; the water would have roared over their voices. Finally, when her teeth had begun to chatter and her nose was numb, her father stopped.

The trail led onward, disappeared into the water. Icrane looked at her. The distant Healer's face changed abruptly; he touched her and smiled, put his mouth close to her ear, and she felt herself relax a little.

"Don't be frightened. The River will not hurt you." He smoothed her hair, straightened a few feathers. Then he put two skins into her hands, one dyed red, one white. "Drink from the white one. It carries your dreams. You know what to do with the red one?" She nodded. "Don't drink the wrong one." He turned her toward the trail's ending. "Don't worry. Dream a happy dream and come back when you're ready. Go, now."

But I'm starving, she thought, for she hadn't been permitted to eat, *and cold, and I'm not sleepy. I don't like being betrothed.* The trail ascended easily, levelled behind the Falls. She stepped between two walls, one black, hard, gleaming like night, one made of

endlessly falling ribbons of light. She thought instantly, *I wish Terje were here to see this.*

The cave was a bubble of darkness. As she walked
into it, the Fall's voice dwindled. A single flame, lit
by her father, floated atop oil filling a natural crevice.
As her eyes adjusted to the different light, she saw
what patterned the rock above the fire, and she
stopped, whispering, "Oh." The marks of the
dreamers, the betrothed . . . There was an animal
skin on the floor. She sat down on it. All her fear had
vanished, and she felt at ease there, belonging there.
She held her hands to the flame, warming them, and
then she uncorked the white skin. The taste of the wine
was hot and sweet, tinged with herbs. She felt her
face flush, and then her hands. She smiled drowsily
on the soft fur, wondering for the first time where her
betrothed was hidden, what ceremony he might be
going through. *Will we like each other?* she wondered. *Will he be like Terje? Will he listen to my
stories?* She finished the wine slowly. The water fell
constantly in front of her. Her eyes began to follow
it, catching one star-gleam of spray, falling with it
into nothingness, catching another, until the sheer
power of the endless falling made her shift, blinking,
trying to imagine what huge world of water lay on
top of the Face, pouring itself day and night into the
River without emptying. *Where does it all come from?*
she wondered. And then she fell asleep.

She dreamed a hundred young girls, dressed as she
was, came out of the shadows of the cave to touch her
face with hands soft as moth wings. She dreamed a
boy's face, dark, unfamiliar, with a deer-sign on his

13

forehead, and she said apologetically to the ghosts, *No, sorry, that's someone else's dream.* A dream already dreamed. She saw the moon and the Moon-Flash. Then she saw the strange Hunter, gazing up at the moon. O point O point O . . . the Face. Her dream went dark, then, evening-dark, silent, breathless. A star exploded in the darkness. She stirred, murmuring. Everything was white. There were no familiar faces. A star was carrying her to the moon. The moon was huge, full, rising toward the Flash. In another moment it would come, in another . . . She looked back down to the Face where a betrothal ceremony was to be held, and she called to the upturned faces: *Farewell. But wait,* she thought in her sleep, *whose dream is this? I'm Kyreol.* Then she saw a hundred rainbows . . . And then only dream fragments.

She woke up. Her arm was cramped against the stone. Her head felt stuffed with feathers, and she was thirsty. She pushed herself up to a sitting position and blinked a moment. The light had shifted away from the falls in front of her, and she knew she had slept for hours. But what a strange dream. Neither happy nor sad. A puzzle. She stood up slowly, straightening her clothes, wishing she could see if the paint had smeared on her face. She frowned at the flame, thinking of the dream, until she remembered the girls' faces, painted, smiling, their soft touches, and she smiled, the first excitement quivering in her. *I am one of you.* She reached for the red skin, poured its contents into a little shallow in the rock that was colored and flecked from the contents of many other skins. She placed her left hand flat in the cold dye. Then, choosing her spot carefully, she put her handprint among the hundreds of gold handprints that rose like butterflies on the black wall above the flame.

I, Kyreol.

She walked out of the cave, caught water in her hands. She washed, then drank deeply, clearing her head. A mixture of excitement and hunger welled through her as she made her way back down the trail. *Now the night can come,* she thought, walking out of the shadow of the Face into the tender, late afternoon light. The night, the Moon-Flash, the feast, the handclasp, the eyes meeting hers out of another mask of paint, a hood of feathers . . . And then the hundred wild red birds freed . . . *Kyreol of Turtle-Crossing. I will live with Korre among the turtles.*

There was feasting when she returned, pregnant with her secret betrothal dream. The falls turned grey, then a feathery silver as the moon rose. It was full, blazing white, its light swallowing the stars around it. A perfect moon, ripe for the fire-flash that would bring good hunting, good harvest, good fortune in marriage. Two great fires were lit: one for her, one for her betrothed, who sat, a bird-child with a turtle on his forehead, on a skin decorated with feathers. She glanced across at him occasionally, wondering what he had dreamed. They would tell each other later. She was surrounded by women, but Terje came among them briefly, bringing her a leaf full of honeyberries. They shared them in silence, while the moon crept upward in the night toward the flash-point. Kyreol, watching the fire, saw in her mind the arrow of fire that carressed so swiftly, so brightly, the curve of the moon and disappeared. "What is it?" she whispered. "The Moon-Flash?"

"It's fire," Terje said softly. "It's a tree, an animal, the River. It's the way the world is."

"But—"

"You can divide water into its smallest piece, and it will still be water. You don't ask what it is. The world is like water. It is just itself."

But, she thought, not even knowing what she was trying to argue about. They finished the berries in silence, close to each other as they had always been. Terje tossed the leaf into the fire. They watched it turn into flame and smoke.

"You see? Everything is one thing: there are only different shapes of it."

Then he kissed her on the cheek, something he had never done before, and rose. The women laughed at him; he went away scowling. Kyreol's thoughts returned to the boy beside the other fire.

As the moon neared the center of a square of stars, a silence fell. Kyreol and Korre were led from their fires to a carpet of skins and feathers, with all the River-signs, and the River itself woven into it. It was very old; newer River-signs had been added on since it was first made. Kyreol's father joined their hands. Korre's hand was sweaty; he glanced at her once, nervously, and smiled. She felt odd, suddenly, restless: she wanted to be climbing a tree or fishing. Then she remembered her new face, the mask of womanhood, and the thought passed. The moon floated into its position.

A chant started, led by her father. A prayer for good fortune. Her name and Korre's name were repeated many times, until it seemed that even the constant roar of the Falls echoed their names. The whole world was chanting. And the flash, the spark of life, entered the moon.

The chanting turned to cheers. Wood pipes and drum sounded out of the night. A hundred birds wove into the firelight, soared upward, singing. Korre let go of Kyreol's hand. His feet shifted. He was still smiling, but he couldn't seem to speak. *Oh well*, Kyreol thought after a moment. *I can talk enough for two.* She looked around vaguely at all the laughing people who seemed to have forgotten about them. At the edge of her fire she saw the hooded Hunter.

She gazed at him, puzzled without knowing why. Then the carpet rose under her as many hands lifted it. She grabbed at Korre and lost her balance. They tumbled against one another, as the carpet shook, and fell, tangled together and laughing.

2

BEING BETROTHED, Kyreol discovered, was not quite as interesting as she had imagined it. For one thing, her face hadn't changed. When she stepped out the door of the house at Turtle-Crossing and knelt at the riverbank to see her reflection, it was still the same face under the paint as the one she had worn at her father's house. For another thing, betrothed women didn't fish. And for another, she and Korre seemed to speak two entirely different languages.

Since she wasn't married yet, she slept with Korre's younger sisters, in the huge, rambling stone house. She liked the house. There was always a stray noise in it—a pot banging, a child laughing or crying, Korre's mother singing or calling to her children. Kyreol helped her with the cooking and took care of the younger children. She had never done either thing in her life, so for a while she was intrigued. She learned how to make fish soup and grind nuts into flour and to save all the feathers she plucked from birds for the many betrothal skirts the family would need. She showed the children how to crack seed pods in two to make tiny boats, and she told them stories. She told about the First Man and the First Woman, and about the First Days of the World, when the fish could talk. She made them tell her what the birds were saying. Korre's mother listened with an indulgent smile, but Korre didn't understand.

"Fish never had voices," he said one evening, when they were sitting on the bank cleaning fish he had caught.

"But why not? Everything else does. Everything in the world makes a noise but fishes. Why?"

"They don't have tongues."

"But—"

He sighed. "You always say 'but.' The world is the world. It's silly to think about fish speaking. You shouldn't say that to the children."

"But why—"

"There you go again."

"I had a thought," she said, prickling with frustration, "and you made it vanish out of my head. Listen. Everything—"

"Kyreol—"

"You never listen to me!"

"Well, you never make any sense!"

Kyreol swallowed her words, sat smoldering. Korre watched her, his chin on his fist. He was shorter than she was, and she was still growing. They had to sit down to look straight into each other's eyes. He was night-dark, muscular but small-boned. He made her feel gawky. He was even-tempered but very stubborn. When she got angry, he only waited calmly, silently, until she gave up her anger, and then he would talk about something entirely different. She waited for him to speak. The River made soft, soothing noises, cooling her. He reached out finally, touched her.

"Do you like me?" he asked. She forgot her anger, surprised that he had said something she could understand.

"Of course I do," she said. "But—"

He threw up his hands, and she swallowed the rest of her thought.

She tried to see the world the way he saw it. A fish was to be eaten. A bird feather was to be used for rituals. People were to worship the River and the Moon-Flash, and rear other people to do the same. It was very simple. Maybe part of becoming a woman was to see the world through simpler eyes. But her brain was always humming like a beehive with questions and possibilities, and there seemed no way to quiet it.

She never thought about Terje, except to wish he was beside her, sometimes, when she saw a stone flecked with tiny stars of light, or a green beetle that looked like a leaf. Or did the leaf look like the beetle? Which came first, the beetle or the leaf? The entire world was full of puzzles. Or maybe it wasn't. Korre never saw anything to be puzzled by. Terje accepted the world the way it was, but he saw the things that Kyreol saw, and he had loved her stories. They only bored Korre. *Oh well*, she thought, *this is the way the world is*. But one morning, as she and Korre's oldest sister, who was on the verge of becoming a woman, took the younger ones down to the river to bathe, Kyreol thought up one question too many.

"Who will you be betrothed to?" she asked Korre's

sister. The girl, who was small and quiet like Korre, and very pretty, glanced at Kyreol shyly.

"Terje."

Kyreol dropped the two small hands she was holding and went back to Turtle-Crossing and climbed the highest tree she could find. She sat there all morning, throwing seed pods in the River, while first Korre's sister and the children, then Korre himself called to her.

"Kyreol! Come down!"

She shook her head mutely. Their voices meant no more to her than bird voices. *Something is wrong*, she kept thinking. *I'm supposed to be happy. This is the way the world is*. Korre wouldn't go fishing until she came down; she wouldn't come down. Korre's mother finally came out and scolded them both. Kyreol climbed down resignedly, and Korre went off in his boat. But he wouldn't take her with him. The deep green River flowed past her feet, freely and slowly, and she, with the little ones tugging at her skirt, could only watch it.

One morning not long afterward, she woke up with tears on her face. She couldn't remember what she had dreamed, so Korre's mother sent her upriver to visit her father. He would sleep for her, dream her dream, understand the message of her sorrow. Then he would tell her dream to the River, and the River would bear it away. Her mind would be peaceful again, as all things in the Riverworld were meant to be.

The sight of the small dark house with its inverted bowls of rooms seemed strange to her. She no longer belonged in it; it was a piece of her past. But she was happy to see her father.

"I saw you coming," he said simply, as he hugged her.

"On the River?"

"In a dream."

He made her sit down in his Healing room, brought her smoked fish and fruit and herb tea. She felt peaceful there, surrounded by River-signs woven of reeds, animal skins, feather-charms, jars of herbs. The River water lapped against the stones under the window; she heard birds singing, not children wailing. Her father touched her cheek.

"You're growing tall."

"Too tall. Korre will have trouble catching up to me."

"He will." He paused. "Are you happy there?"

"Oh, yes." She sighed. "But—" She caught herself and laughed. "Korre doesn't like me to say 'but.' " She was silent, then, for a long while. She said softly, "Will you dream for me?"

His face darkened a little, but not with anger. "Why?"

"I want—I want to be happy. I'm trying to be happy. I want to know that I will be."

He gazed at her, his eyes like birds' eyes, steady and unwinking. Looking back at him, she sensed suddenly the long, changeless past of the Riverworld, its names, its rituals, its Healers. One year was like any year; one Moon-Flash was every Moon-Flash. A man would die on one part of the River, but someone else would be born on another part to take his place. She herself was every woman; her growing, her betrothal no different than a woman's in the past or a woman to be born. She was part of the River, flowing into her place as the fish and the trees flowed into theirs. There was no need for her to think about being happy, any more than a bird thought about it. The moon never questioned the moon-fire; the fish never questioned their voicelessness.

But.

She stirred restively, pulling away from her father's eyes. He looked down. She put her hands to her mouth, for his face had become open, vulnerable, confused, as if somehow she had hurt him.

"What is it?" she whispered. "What did I do?"

He shook his head. "I don't know. There is a strangeness in you . . ."

Her eyes filled with tears. "I don't want to be strange! Is it because I tell stories? Korre says that's what's wrong with me."

"No, no . . ." He put his hand on her knee, his face easing again, smiling a little. "I like your stories. And Korre tells himself stories every night in his dreams."

"He dreams about fishing. Will you dream for me?"

"No."

"But why? You would for anyone else."

He brushed her cheek again. "It's a simple reason. I could dream for you, but I think I would not understand the dream." She opened her mouth to argue, but he held up his hand. "No. You are a Healer's daughter, and you will see into your own dreaming better than I could."

"But—"

He laughed and poured her more tea.

She went back home to Turtle-Crossing the next

day. The children gathered around her; she picked up two of them in her strong arms and realized she enjoyed the feel of them. Korre was happy to see her.

"Did you dream?" he asked eagerly, for maybe now she would be content and not argue so much. Kyreol, looking at him, lied for the first time in her life.

"Yes," she said gruffly.

"What was the dream?"

"I dreamed of the River-tree. I was homesick." It was on the tip of her tongue to invent a more interesting dream, but Korre liked simple things, so she didn't. He smiled, pleased, then lifted his face unexpectedly to kiss her cheek. Then he began to talk about his catch, not noticing how she had drawn back from him, startled, sensing dimly how many lies she might have to tell for the rest of her life to keep him happy.

A few days later, she saw Terje. He was poling their boat down the lazy, sandy section at Turtle-Crossing. She was on the bank a ways from the house, digging for turtle eggs. He had the prow of the boat resting on the sand before she noticed him.

She straightened. He seemed a piece of her past, too, like her father's house, only half-familiar. He dug his pole into the sand and jumped out, narrowly missing her egg basket. He had to look up at her a little more than before. That made her want to laugh suddenly, and her smile made him real, not a memory. He didn't smile; he was scowling, at her or the hot sun, she couldn't tell. Then she remembered who he was betrothed to, and she stopped smiling. She bent down, dug in the sand, not looking at him.

"Kyreol."

"What?"

He didn't say what, just stood there. She glanced at him finally. The rich, tawny gold of his skin made her blink, and she thought, *We're different colors, like the birds. I wonder* . . . But she stifled the question, since there were no answers, and uncovered a nest in the sand. He squatted down, helped her put the eggs in the basket.

She said again, "What?"

He sighed. "Nothing." Then he added, "I wish you could go fishing with me."

"I don't fish anymore," she said with dignity. "I cook, I make clothes, I take care of the children— Why," she asked irritably, meeting his eyes finally, "didn't you tell me you were betrothed to Korre's sister?"

He shrugged, surprised. "I forgot. She was never in my mind."

"Well, she's going to be at the next Moon-Flash. She became a woman last month." He made a noncommital grunt; she added severely, "That seems like a long time to you. Forever until Moon-Flash. But it's not, it's—"

"I know. But why are you angry? That's the way things are."

She resisted an impulse to dump the turtle eggs on his head. She turned away instead, searched for another nest. He watched her silently awhile. Then he said softly, "Do you miss me?"

"No. I have Korre, I have a new family. That's the way the world is."

"Do you tell him stories?"

"No. The stories are for children."

He was silent again, gazing down at the empty nest. He said finally, "You used to laugh more. If I were betrothed to you, I'd make you come fishing. I'd make you sit beside me in a tree and talk to me about the world, because no one else sees it the way you do. Sometimes—sometimes I think if you looked enough and talked enough, you'd turn the world into a different shape, a shape I've never seen before. But . . ." He scooped sand up in his hand, let it trickle out between his fingers. "There was not enough time. I think about you. Sometimes I dream about you, trying to tell me something." He brushed his hand clean on his thigh and stood up. She stared at his back as he went to the boat, her hands frozen in the sand. His name filled her throat, like a story that ached to be told. The ghost of a younger Kyreol tugged at her, yearning to be free to follow him. But there was no place in the world for such freedom. She stayed still, her bones heavy, too heavy to move. He shoved the boat out, poled away without looking back. Her hands moved finally; she looked down dully and found more eggs.

At the sixth full moon from Moon-Flash time, there was another ritual. This was in honor of the River, which fed them, accepted their dead, wound through their lives and their dreams. Kyreol sat down with the youngest children under a tree and explained to them what would happen, for it was a solemn ritual, and very long.

"The Healer—my father—rows a boat out to the middle of the River—"

"At Turtle-Crossing?"

"Near River-Tree. Upriver, where it's slow and broad. In the boat there are two big stones tied to vines. He throws the stones into the water, and the boat is anchored there. My father is all dressed in the winter skins of animals. He holds fire in one hand and water in the other. A torch and a bowl. Now . . ." She hushed her voice, and the children, clinging to her knees, leaned closer to her. "The moon has set behind the Face, and the world is very dark. My father begins to chant. He says all the names of the living—your names, too. Then he says all the names of the dead that the River has carried away. Then—now, this is a hard part, so listen carefully—he draws all the River-signs on the water with his torch. He makes reflections with fire of the River-Tree, Turtle-Crossing, Little Spring, so that the River will recognize and remember all our signs. Then, when he finishes, he drinks the water in the bowl, and he throws the torch into the water. So then it is very dark." She paused dramatically. A child whispered,

"Then what does he do?"

"He waits. We all wait."

"In the dark?"

"Yes."

"For what?"

"For the sun!" Her fingers swooped down, tickling, and the children bumped against her, giggling helplessly. "Then the happy part begins. Everyone throws gifts into the River—nuts, flowers, feathers—anything that will float. Then there are boat races, as people follow the gifts, to see which the River accepts first, which are snagged, which ones are rejected and washed ashore, which ones keep floating in the sunlight down to the end of the world. Then we all give presents to each other and eat until we can't eat one

27

more bite, then we sail back to bed and dream good dreams."

Kyreol showed the children how to make bracelets of grass and flowers for the River. She made amulets for her father and Korre, circles of leather with their signs painted on them. She made a seed bracelet for Korre's mother and a feather armband for Korre's father. She spent two days helping cook for the feast: nut bread, fish stew, shellfish seasoned with herbs, stuffed turtle eggs. On the afternoon before the ritual, she took a basket into the forest to gather musk-berries, which smelled like dead fish, but turned tart and sparkling when you bit into them.

She found them easily by their smell, which even the birds avoided. She was picking them happily, enjoying the warm ground under her bare feet, the lazy, quiet breezes, when suddenly, for no reason at all, her happiness turned upside-down inside her and dissolved into a rainstorm of misery. She dropped the basket, sat down in the crook of a tree, and cried like a baby, noisily and desperately, without even knowing why. And as she cried, all the questions she had ever asked came flooding back to her.

What shape is the world?

Where does the River go?

What lies before the Face, beyond Fourteen Falls?

Did my mother go into a dream? Or did she go beyond the Riverworld?

What are the sun and the stars and the world?

What is the Moon-Flash?

She stayed under the tree until the world was black. Once she heard voices calling her from a distance: Kyreol! Kyreol! But she didn't move. *This is my time,* she thought. *My time for thinking.* As the thin moon edged upward, she felt an older and younger Kyreol, herself before she had put on the betrothal mask: lean and restive and curious, wondering about lights and shadows, full of tales. A wind whispered among the trees. *Is it the dead? Do they change shape, as Terje says, into water and wind? Do they speak, like fish, with voices we can't hear?*

She rose finally, feeling full of night and wind, and walked silently as an animal down to the River. Her father was there, a torchlight figure standing in the black ritual boat, gazing down at the water. The banks were crowded with people. She took her place among them unnoticed. The Healer was in the middle of the death chant, naming, sign by sign, family by family, those the River had carried away. When he came to the River-Tree sign, she listened carefully. Her mother's name was not among them. The wind blew the torch-fire into a long blazing ribbon over the water. Finally, hours later it seemed, the torch flew like a star into the water, and the River accepted it.

They waited. The moon set; the world was very dark. The stars faded. Little by little, the winds blew the darkness away, blew in the delicate greys and misty purples of dawn. Kyreol stirred a little, blinking, wondering finally where her Turtle-Crossing family was. Not far from her, still as a tree shadow beneath a tree on the bank, stood the Hunter.

She moved when he moved, swiftly, soundlessly, without questioning herself. *He knows something,* she thought. *He knows.* He went straight into the forest, away from the people and the sunrise. *He doesn't want to be seen, he doesn't want the sun to see him. Why?*

He drew her deeper into the trees, then made a wide circle back to the bank and headed upriver. She ducked from tree to tree along the bank, keeping him in sight; the water, quickened from its journey down the Face, hid the sound of her following. He rounded a fall of boulders beside the River and seemed to disappear. But she and Terje had explored every secret place on the River they could find. She slipped into a crevice between two great boulders and found him standing in an eerie light, speaking again to his stone.

They stared at one another, Kyreol and the Hunter. He was wearing skins now instead of feathers, and he had a bone knife in his thigh-band. But there was no River-sign on it.

She took a step toward him. The Falls boomed in the distance; the swift water churned past the boulders. The River-voice was strong, tangling in her thoughts. For a moment his face was expressionless, dark as the rock of the Face. Then he took a silent breath. The stone clicked in his hand, opened. He said one word to it.

"Interface."

3

"WHO ARE YOU?" Kyreol whispered. He held up his palm, showing her the Hunter's wavy River-sign on it. His eyes were flat, telling her nothing.

'Why did you follow me?"

"I want to know about the world."

He made an arc in the air with his hand. "The River is the world."

She gazed at him. He looked like a hunter, lean and muscular, with his good-luck stone in his hand and a knife he hadn't finished carving at his thigh. Hunters were often solitary people, ranging the forests at will, only seen when they brought in their skins and meat, or at rituals. She shifted a little, perplexed. Then the true inner feeling she had about him welled up in her again, and she took a step toward him.

"Then where did my mother go?"

"What?"

"My father said he dreamed my mother found a beautiful stone that opened and said her name, and then she went away. Is that the stone?"

The Hunter's hand tightened on the stone. "He dreamed—"

"It was a stone like a star."

"This is my hunting stone. My fortune." Then he asked slowly, "What is your mother's name?"

"Nara. Of River-Tree and Turtle-Crossing. Everyone knew her."

He stood very still. He seemed to have withdrawn into himself, like water seeping into earth, leaving only his shape, motionless, shadow-dark, which a grazing animal would hardly notice. She took a small step forward, her voice small in his silence.

"Please. Please tell me. I want to know so many things. I want to—"

"Go back," he said brusquely. "Go back to the rituals. Your answers are there."

"No!" she cried despairingly. "There's only one answer: 'This is the way the world is.' But it doesn't tell me about the world. What makes trees grow, why birds and people are different colors, where the River comes from, where it goes, what the Moon-Flash is. If you don't tell me, I'll go back to Korre and have babies, and I'll tell them stories, but I'll never know anything, never."

He didn't move; he almost didn't seem to be breathing. "I am a hunter. Why do you ask me these things? You should ask the Healer."

"I've heard you speak to your stone. You know words my father doesn't know. You know—" She stopped, watching the expression well into his eyes. "You know," she whispered.

He was silent for a long time. He was the Hunter, but something in his face made her feel that she had trapped him and he could not escape. He shifted finally, looking completely bewildered, and asked gently, "Who are you?"

"Kyreol, of River-Tree and Turtle-Crossing. You saw me betrothed."

"Oh, yes. Your face was painted then; I didn't recognize you."

"What does 'interface' mean?"

"It means—it means two worlds touching. Yours and mine. It means I may not be able to return to the Riverworld, now that you've seen me."

"Why?" she asked puzzledly. "Are you a ghost? Are you from a dream?"

He smiled. "No."

"Then where are you from?"

He gazed at her again, silently. Then he squatted down, drew a circle with his fingers on the sandy floor of the cave. "This is the world."

"It is round!" Then she asked suspiciously, "Is it flat-round, or round like a berry?"

"Like a berry." He drew the wavy line she recognized down the center of the world. "This is the River."

"I know." She touched the top of the world. "And this is the Face."

"No." He made a tiny dot halfway to the center of the world. "The Face is here." He made another tiny dot, very close to the first dot. "There is Fourteen Falls."

"Wait—" she whispered. His hand stopped. She was shaking her head; her body made a step back from him. "Nothing can be that big. It's only a tale, you dreamed it."

He opened his hand quickly, brushed the world away and rose. "It's only a dream," he said gently. "I am a hunter. Go back to the ritual. You will never see me again. I am part of the dream."

She stared down at the sand where his drawing had been. "Past Fourteen Falls. Are there other place-names? What—what is the name of the place you came from?"

He was motionless again before her, a hunter, another teller of tales. "The River is the world. There is nothing beyond Fourteen Falls."

She stood staring at the sand where he had left his handprint long after he had gone.

The sun had risen; she could hear shouting and laughter from the distance. She walked back down the River slowly, thinking, *It is true. It isn't true. But he knew where my mother went. I could see that in his eyes. He is a hunter, he is a dream. The world is little. The world is huge. I forgot to ask him what the Moon-Flash is.* She didn't realize she was back among people until Korre shouted at her.

"Kyreol! Kyreol!" He ran to her, threw a necklace of flowers over her head, and kissed her cheek. "Where have you been?"

"Here," she said simply, because the world was either so huge there was no room for "here" and "there" in their tiny piece of it, or else the River was the World, and everywhere was "here." Korre shook his head bewilderedly.

"No one could find you."

"I was thinking."

"Oh." He still looked puzzled, but he ignored the

puzzlement. "Did you get the musk-berries? Come and eat—" He put his arm around her, but she stood still, pulling against him.

"I'm not hungry. I'm still thinking."

"Kyreol . . ."

She shrugged him away, suddenly irritable. "You go eat."

"No," he said calmly. "You come with me. I want you with me."

"Korre—"

"You are betrothed. This is ritual-time. I want you with me."

She eyed him. His face was young and stubborn. She wondered what it would look like old and stubborn. His voice would be deep; he would be taller than she. *Kyreol. Come with me.* She would have no reason to argue, for the Hunter was gone forever and even his handprint would be brushed away by the footprints of other curious children. He was no dream, she knew. He had drawn her a picture of the world and then gone somewhere into it. Somewhere past Fourteen Falls, beyond the Face.

"Kyreol."

"Wait," she pleaded. "I want to see my father. I haven't given him his gift yet. You eat. I'll join you—"

"I'll go with you."

She swallowed an exasperated sigh. If she had to live with him, she might as well do it peacefully "Korre," she said very patiently, "I am a Healer's daughter. Sometimes I see things, and then I have to be alone to think about them."

Unexpectedly, that made sense to him. "All right," he said reluctantly, "but come back soon."

"I will." She kissed his cheek suddenly, surprising both of them. "Save me some turtle eggs."

He smiled at her shyly, pleased. "I will. Hurry."

She walked through the crowd without seeing her father. She didn't really want to talk to him anyway; he didn't know how to draw her a picture of the world. The River was full of children's rafts following the floating gifts. They passed her noisily, shouting, splashing, pushing each other into the water. The River carried them away finally. She reached her favorite place on the bank near her father's house and sat down in a coil of tree roots to think.

A little while later, she stirred and threw a stone in the water. Thinking did no good whatsoever. Then, unexpectedly, the River sent her a gift. She cupped her hands to her mouth and called, "Terje!"

He was sailing past her, stalking a River-gift, in the boat that they had made. When he saw her, he angled the boat in the current, poled over to her. His face seemed odd to her, distant, as if he had forgotten her name, and the strange jumble of things she wanted to tell him dwindled away. The River-gift, a necklace of seed pods, drifted past them.

He jumped off the boat and pulled it partway up the bank, his head turned toward the gift. "It's Jage's gift. She wanted me to see how far it went."

"Oh," Kyreol said. Jage was Terje's betrothed. She assumed dignity, her shoulders drawing back, her chin lifting, though she felt suddenly lonely. He looked at her finally.

"What?"

"Oh. Nothing."

"Well, what? You called me."

"I just wanted to tell you something. But it doesn't matter. You have Jage to think about now."

He gazed at her, his face puckering in bewilderment. "What did you want to tell me?"

"I need to use the boat. That's all. But we can follow Jage's gift first." She climbed in. "Hurry. You can still see it. It's important, too. Maybe more important, if you're right about everything. The world will be as you see it."

He got in beside her, shoved the boat away from the bank with his pole. "Kyreol—"

"Her handprint will be on that wall, next Moon-Flash. She'll come to live with you. That's the way things should be."

"Kyreol—"

"I'm just going for a little way. Then I'll be back."

They caught the current again. The seed pods spun gently in an eddy, then drew them on. Terje poled to catch up with them. "What," he demanded, "are you talking about? How far are you going?"

"Just a little way. To Fourteen Falls."

He stared at her, his face blank with astonishment, clinging so long to the pole he nearly fell overboard. "That's the end of the world!"

She stood like a dark figurehead at the prow of the boat, turned backward, saying goodbye to her world, or maybe only leaving it so that she could greet it again. "Kyreol . . . of River-Tree and Turtle-Crossing," she whispered, so not to forget. Behind her, the River-gift of Terje's betrothed caught in a snag and stopped moving. Terje lifted the pole out of the water and sat down.

"Can we be back by Moon-Flash?"

"Of course," she said, annoyed. "You won't miss your betrothal." Then, listening to his words, she smiled.

4

FOURTEEN FALLS, the River's end, was the birth-place of all the rainbows in the world. They grew like seedlings in the water, blossomed, and when they reached their full size, detached themselves and drifted through the world. Long ago, during a terrible famine, a hunter had strayed too far downriver, farther than anyone had ever gone, and he had seen more rainbows than he could count. He had broken his bow so, braving the wild currents, he had picked a small rainbow and strung it. Wherever he shot his arrows, they struck plump birds and beasts, until he had enough food to feed everyone in the Riverworld. Since then, a rainbow meant good luck to whoever saw it, and hunters carved rainbows on their bows in memory of the first man who had plucked the magic out of Fourteen Falls.

Terje and Kyreol got to the rainbow garden at the end of the world much faster than they expected to.

On the first day, the River took them at a leisurely pace past all the place-names they knew. Most of the houses stood empty, sunning their round baked walls like mud turtles in the light. At Little Spring an old man, who was too frail to make the journey to the ritual-place, bent over his fishlines, catching his supper. He wore the mark of a silver stream on his forehead and a black feather for the dead tucked behind his ear. He waved to them, smiling, his black face wrinkled like water. *Farewell*. Kyreol waved back. The River bore them onward.

The current quickened; by midday they no longer needed to pole. Kyreol took the rudder and Terje baited fishlines, trailed them from the stern. Then he sat beside Kyreol and unwrapped a leaf full of nut bread, which he had taken from the feast. They ate it together.

"Why?"

"Why what?" Kyreol said with her mouth full.

"Why are we going to Fourteen Falls?"

She told him about the Hunter. He listened silently, without eating, his eyes big, dark in his face. When she finished, his throat made a noise, as if to clear away a breadcrumb. He opened his mouth, then turned as his fishline twitched. He pulled the fish in. "It's a dream . . ." he whispered. "It's a Hunter's dream. It means something to him, and he gave it to you, the Healer's daughter."

"Maybe," Kyreol said doubtfully. "But I think it's not a dream."

"It's a dream." His voice came back again, flicking away her uncertainty the way the fish, trapped in his hand, was flicking droplets off its scales. He eased it into a clay water jar. "You're just not old enough to know what it means."

She scowled at his complacency. "Then why are you coming with me?"

"To see the rainbows, of course."

By late afternoon the place-names grew few. Only hunters lived so far from the Face. Black Cove, Flower Marsh, Sun's Carpet, the clearing where hunters cured hides, swept past them. The River narrowed; its voice began to rumble. When the world grew dark, they tied the boat to a tree. Terje made a fire from the spark in his oil lantern and cooked the fish. They ate, then slept on the boat under the icy shower of stars.

The next afternoon they left the forests behind. The River seemed to burrow downward into the stony heart of the world. Where the soft bank had been, steep shining walls of black rock rose high above them. The thunder of water bounced from wall to wall and echoed all around them. Kyreol felt uneasy, but Terje, handling the rudder, his hair wet with spray, was grinning. He swung the bow away from a patch of rocks that had grown abruptly out of the water and Kyreol slid to the bottom of the boat.

He shouted, "The pole!"

Lifting her head, she stared down a toothy corridor of rocks. The breath left her; Terje yelled exuberantly. She scrambled to her feet, wielding the pole like a weapon against the black teeth. The bow tilted, and down they went, faster than she had ever gone anywhere, into a froth and roar of water. And suddenly, dancing from rock to rock, there were the rainbows.

"Oh, Terje!"

"Rock!"

"Look at that!"

"Ow!"

"I'm sorry—"

"Rock! Sunside!"

She swung the pole, narrowly missing his head again. It was magic. If she looked ahead, there were no rainbows, just the steep glittering path. If she glanced behind there were rainbows. Everywhere. More than fourteen. A hundred—huge rainbows spanning the river, tiny flames of rainbows spanning the white flow of water between two rocks. They swooped down into a deep pool. The water slowed briefly, and Terje looked behind them, laughing at the airy gateways of color they had come through. Then his head snapped around.

Something grabbed at the boat from beneath, knocking him to the floor. Kyreol shrieked. Down they went again, the safe green pool only a memory. Terje dove for the rudder. The boat tilted, seemed to hang in midair for a moment, then hit the water with a smack. The fish pot spilled; the oil lamp went overboard. Kyreol's stomach lurched.

"Terje—"

"Rock!"

There were rocks on all sides. Kyreol pushed against the biggest with all her strength; the boat swung away from it and another mountain of rock grazed their side. She wanted to close her eyes, let the river jostle them, spin them, turn them upside-down and inside-out, and cast them finally into some quiet depth. But Terje was still steering and yelling at her. The boat jumped like a fish over another fall and turned sideways.

"Push!" Terje gasped. "Push!"

42

She pushed the pole against a rock, and the boat turned backwards. She saw the rainbows again, burning in the sunset. Something tore against the underside of the boat. Then the river disappeared again.

"Terje!" she wailed. The boat shot into midair, spun over, and tossed them out like dolls into deep water.

She went down and down into a grey, raging storm. The River was the world, and the world was a heaving, whirling force, a wilderness of water. It spat her back into the air before she drowned, and she glimpsed the swift, sudden clouds gathering overhead. A rock loomed in front of her. She groped at it; it slid away under her fingers, and the boiling water dragged her under again. The River seemed huge suddenly, swollen beyond its banks. There was no life in it, no fish, no waterweeds, only its own restless, turbulent life. She reached the surface again. Lightning ripped across the swollen clouds; thunder beat at her ears. *The River is angry*, she thought, trying to swim, but there seemed no place to swim to. The whole world was water. *Am I dreaming?* she wondered. *Am I dead?* Pulling herself to the surface again, she tried to see Terje. But rain was pouring out of the clouds, biting her face, and she dove down under again. A long, mournful *Terje!* wailed through her. Half-swimming, half-pulled by the strange, dark waters, she felt hopelessly adrift in a new world, a nameless place with no rainbows and no human faces.

Finally, when nothing seemed to exist at all but night and water, when she felt ready to let the River take her, turn her into a piece of itself, she felt a stone bump her knee. She put her hand down onto mud and rocks, then pulled herself forward onto the shores of the world, into the rain and wild lightning, and fell asleep.

Someone was shaking her. She lifted her head groggily and spit out a few grains of silt. She put her face down again, wanting to go back to sleep, but the hand shook her again.

"Kyreol."

She opened her eyes, groaning a protest. The sky swam soggily overhead, swollen and grey. A stray raindrop smacked her cheek. The stormy river flooded through her memory, and she sat up abruptly, remembering where she was.

"Terje . . ."

He had moved away from her to the bank; he was gazing downriver. They were on a small, sandy wedge of bank, enclosed by jagged cliffs. The River, spilling down from the Falls, had grown enormous.

"Terje," she whispered. He couldn't have heard her, but he turned. His eyes were wide, startled. *Wherever the world ends*, they told her silently, *it doesn't end at Fourteen Falls.* He came back to her side. His skin was scratched, and his hair was matted with sand on one side where he had lain. She felt her own tangled hair. The seed necklace Korre had made for her was gone. Her clothes were torn, her knees were scraped, and her head felt stuffed. She could see the last of the Falls they had gone over, but in the grey sheen of spray she couldn't see a single rainbow.

Rain gusted over them. Terje tugged at her arm; she rose stiffly. They crouched at the cliff edge, shivering.

"Kyreol," Terje said. He had to put his face close to hers to be heard over the roar of water. He was shielding her face partway with his arm, but the rain ran like a waterfall down his own face.

"What?"

"Who was that hunter?"

She shook her head bewilderedly. He had come into her life and gone, and because of him they were drowning in a squall on a spit of sand someplace beyond the edge of the world.

Terje said glumly into her ear, "We lost the boat. I saw it break."

"I wish we had the oil lamp."

"I wish we had the fishlines."

"How do you make fire?"

He shrugged. "Hunters know. I don't."

She was silent. There were always bits of fire in oil lamps, in clay ovens and cooking pits, on torches . . . she never had to ask where it came from; it was always there, always burning. If you fed it, it never died, and if yours died, you could ask your neighbor for a piece as big as a thumbnail, and from that tiny flame, you could make fires to warm you for the rest of your life. You could give it away a thousand times and still have it.

"But where did the first flame come from?" She hardly realized she had spoken aloud until she saw the blood rushing into Terje's face. At first she thought he was going to shout, he looked that angry. Then his muscles went limp, and he leaned against the wet cliff, laughing.

She smiled a little, uncertainly, and touched his cheek with one finger. "Your skin changes colors. Mine never does. Don't worry. We can make another boat when the sky clears."

He stared at her. "For what? We'll have to walk home."

"No, so we can—Don't you want to know where the river goes? Where the Hunter came from? Terje—"

He had turned to the cliff and was groping for handholds. "All I want to do," he said, sighing, "is get out of the rain."

The cliffs were bulky, lumpy with handholds. When they were midway to the top, the rain began to pour again, as though the entire world were angry at them. *Did we do wrong?* Kyreol wondered. *Will the River ever be peaceful again?* The rocks grew slippery; her arms shook with weariness. She heard thunder, a deep, reproachful voice out of the sky. Finally they reached the top, and as they stood panting, the air dissolved into grey, pounding sheets of rain.

There were a few trees, another wall of rock in front of them. Terje took Kyreol's wrist, tugged her forward to shelter beside them. She moved mechanically, wondering if this was what birds felt like in the rain: sodden, cold, and blind. Then Terje, groping at the stones, made a noise. He pulled at her again, and suddenly they were out of the rain.

It was dim in the cave, but dry. They sank to the ground, huddling against each other. Rain sluiced in a silvery veil over the mouth of the cave. They shivered until their muscles warmed with exertion, and they could finally stop and listen to the sounds of their teeth chattering.

"Well," Terje said after a while. "I can make vine traps. When the rain stops. When we reach the forest again, I can hunt."

"We can't cook."

"Oh. Well, at least the berries are—"

"Terje. We can't just turn around and go home."

"Yes, we can. We've seen the rainbows. That's enough."

"What about the Hunter? What about my mother?"

"Your mother." His face turned away from the rain; she felt his eyes. There was a note of wariness in his voice. "What about your mother?"

"I think—I think the Hunter knows her."

"Kyreol, you're dreaming!"

"When I said her name, he grew still. So still. As if he held a secret—"

"Maybe he is only a hunter—maybe the world is only a little bit bigger than this, and that was his secret: that he hunts beyond the Falls."

"I don't think so," she whispered. "I think the world is huge. And the River knows it all."

The mouth of the cave turned a strange, violent white, and she jumped. Thunder rattled like boulders over their heads. She flung her arms around Terje, hiding her eyes.

"Did I say something wrong?"

He hugged her comfortingly. "No. It's just the sky making noise."

"How does it do that? Maybe the winds all blow at the same time and crash into each other—"

"Maybe."

"Or maybe—" The lightning flashed again, seemingly at their feet. There was an odd, tearing sound, just before the thunder pounded at their heads again. Kyreol pushed her hands over her ears, squealing. The air smelled peculiar. Then a gust of wind blew through the cave and she coughed on a more familiar smell.

She lifted her head. Terje was already at the cave mouth. "Kyreol!" She stumbled to her feet, peered out. A tree, split by the lightning, was burning its heart out in the rain.

"Fire!"

They dashed out. The fire was struggling against the rain, but they rescued bits of burning splinters, brought them safely into the cave. Kyreol took one of the wood splinters, searched the cave floor for leaves and twigs, while Terje salvaged what he could of the wet blazing wood. Kyreol coaxed the fire anxiously, blowing on it, feeding it tiny dry chips of wood until Terje came in with torches in both hands and the cave swam with heat and light.

He didn't stop until he carried every smoldering branch he could find to the fire. By that time, it was so big it drove them farther into the cave. They sat down then, dirty and streaked with smoke, dazed with warmth. Outside, the rain eased to a steady, constant patter, and the thunder grumbled away into the distance.

"My bones are getting warm," Kyreol murmured drowsily. The cave walls were sparkling with star-flecks of light. "We're the First People, and we discovered fire."

Terje grunted. He watched the fire through slitted eyes, looking half-asleep and dreaming. "That's not how the hunters have to do it. They use a stone that carries fire in it. You strike it, and it sparks. Only first you have to speak to it."

48

"What do you say?"

"You tell it your name, and why you want the fire. Only special stones do that."

"Fire from stone, fire out of the air . . . I thought the world was made of water, but maybe it's made of fire."

"And wind," Terje murmured as it blew rain into the cave mouth. He was lying lazily, his body curved around the warmth. He shifted slightly, brushed a pebble from underneath his ribs. "And rocks."

"Terje, how old do you think the world is?"

"Old."

"Older than the First People? So that when they came, there was already fire to keep them warm, berries to feed them?" She gazed at the fire, seeing the First People in the flames. "Maybe they found fire like we did, a burning tree in the rain . . . I wonder why they called it fire. Terje, if you saw fire for the first time, would you call it fire?"

"No," he said drowsily, "I'd call it berries."

"You would not."

"Or fish. I'm hungry."

"Terje, where do you think words came from?"

"It's easier than drawing a picture every time you want something. Do you want me to listen to you? Or do you want me to go out and look for food?"

"I want you to find the end of the world with me."

"Kyreol—"

"I want to go so far that I won't have any more questions. Then I want to come back to the River-world. The world is round. The Hunter showed me. So any path I take will lead me home."

"The Hunter." He lifted his head, blinking away

his drowsiness. "Kyreol, I think this must be the edge of the world. The Hunter is a dreamer from the Riverworld, like you. Because why would anyone from another world dress like a hunter and pretend to be part of the Riverworld? That doesn't make any sense."

What Terje said made so much sense that Kyreol decided to ignore it. "Well. If you think the world is so small, it will be easy for us to find the end of it. Then we can go back. Will you come?" He was silent; she looked at him but his eyes were turned away from her toward the fire. "Terje," she pleaded softly. "I had a betrothal dream. In it I said goodbye to everyone."

"Kyreol—"

"Please don't make me go alone."

He met her eyes, then. He stretched out his hand, and she reached for it, held it, as she had done years ago when they were children, before she grew so tall. "I don't want you to leave the Riverworld like your mother and not come back," he said gruffly. "I always want to know where you are. You make me see things."

"Terje, how do dreams know?"

He made a shape in the air with his free hand, against the fire and darkness. "Everything is one piece. Even dreams."

"Then," she said, trusting him, "there's no need to be afraid."

He didn't answer. He loosed his hand after a moment and got to his feet. "I'll find some berries," he said. "Watch the fire." At the cave mouth he turned, gazed at it again, reluctant to leave it, remembering the cold. Kyreol said, "Don't worry," and he went out into the rain.

Kyreol stirred stiffly, pulled a twig from the fire. Not all the wishes in the world would keep it going; now that they had light, she could search more carefully for wood. The cave was deeper than she expected. She walked toward the shadows in the back. They parted, revealing not a cave wall, but a curve in the wall leading into more shadows. She hesitated, forgetting the wood, then went down the passage.

The ground was soft, chilly underfoot. There was no sound but her breathing. She walked slowly, peering forward at the tiny ring of light until she realized that a mystery lay not at the edge of the light but all around her on the walls.

She stopped, her breath catching. She raised the light, and a strange animal painted red stared back at her. She moved the light. The sun, the moon, a pattern of stars. Another animal, big, lumbering, with strange teeth. A face painted gold, with an unfamiliar pattern of markings on it. Stick figures fishing in the river, hunting animals. A cliff full of eyes and mouths . . . No. Windows and doors. A village inside the cliffs . . .

Her skin prickled as if a hot wind had blown over her. She said, "Terje," and her voice came tiny and faraway, as if she had spoken in a dream. The paintings grew larger, more elaborate. A man with a fish's head arched over her, his toes on the bottom of one wall, his fingertips touching the bottom of the other. A woman with a sun-head. A huge blue bird, wingtips spanning the walls. How far the passage went, what lay at its end, she didn't know.

People. The word gusted through her like a wind. People not of the Riverworld, who wore strange signs on their faces, different clothing. They had painted the walls and gone away, leaving no footprints, nothing, no one to say why the paintings were there.

"As if," Kyreol whispered, "someone a long time from now walked into the betrothal cave; all she would see is gold hands. A waterfall, a cave, and the gold hands . . . She'd have to tell herself a story . . ." She heard her voice chattering, but she couldn't stop. "The animals are different. They drew the Falls with the rainbows. The River goes on and on, but they never saw the Face . . . There's no story in the Riverworld to explain the paintings. The Hunter wasn't dreaming. The Riverworld is a tiny dream inside the huge world."

The fire ate her twig, began to nibble at her fingers. She turned abruptly, ran back through the silent passageway. "Terje! Terje!"

The twig burned itself out as she ran back into the light. But what she saw there was as incomprehensible as the paintings. There were nuts and berries scattered all around the fire. But no Terje.

5

SHE SEARCHED for him everywhere. She went down the cliff wall and looked for him on the small beach; then, when it was too dark to see, she called him again and again from the cave. Her voice battled the wind mournfully: *Terje!* She kept the fire going all night, waiting for him to return. Near dawn, she fell asleep and dreamed.

She dreamed of the Hunter, standing beside the fire, saying her name again and again. *Kyreol.* He looked at her, but couldn't see her, and she thought in the dream, *I am invisible.* He couldn't hear when she answered, and his voice grew more and more urgent. She woke, trying to speak to him. There were footprints all around the fire.

She got up swiftly. The fire was dead, and she was cold again. The footprints were different sizes; they came into the cave mouth and left by it. *Ghosts,* she thought numbly, even though she knew the dead moved like shadows, disturbing nothing. As she stumbled, half-asleep and bewildered, to the cave mouth, a figure loomed into it, blocking the dawn.

She put her hands over her mouth. A face woven out of reeds, with two square eyes and a slit mouth stared back at her. The rest of the figure was cloaked in black fur. It came toward her, half-crouched, step by slow step. She stood transfixed, her heart hammering. The figure moved closer, leaving human footprints on the ground. When it was almost close enough to touch her, a hand came out of the cloak, shook a string of bones at her.

She squealed, then turned and ran. The painted passageway, which had been so dark at night, was dimly lit with shafts of grey. As she ran down it, her panic mingled with indignation, that a person dressed as a thing had come out of nowhere, stolen Terje away, and then rattled old bones at her. The paintings, muted in the light, swirled past her. Their faces were friendlier, their masks—the fish, the sun—were more cheerful than the gloomy reed-face. She stopped finally, pressed against a crevice, and listened. Then she ran again.

She slowed finally, panting, beginning to cry a little. Reed-Face was still behind her; she heard the rattle of its bones. But she was too tired to run any more, and too upset. She pushed herself into a shadow, tried to become flat, like a painting. The dark figure rounded a corner. Its square eyes peered left, right, then into her still face. She gathered her muscles and sprang at it with a shriek.

The dark cloak, the bones, the mask fell to a heap on the ground. She caught a glimpse of a blue face beneath the mask, and then whoever it was disappeared back down the passageway.

She wiped a tear away angrily and put on the cloak.

54

It was soft and warm, covering her from shoulder to ankle. She hesitated a moment, then picked up the mask, looked at it curiously. It was tightly woven, with a cap attached to keep it on the head. It looked new; some of the reeds were not yet dry. Someone had spent days making it. But why? She gazed at its strange eyes, and it seemed to speak to her.

Why would anyone want to wear a face like yours?

Because, it said, *I make you invisible and you cannot be harmed.*

She put it on. *Now I am Reed-Face*, she thought, and picked up the bones. *No one can scare me again.* She continued down the passageway, not knowing where she was going, but not wanting to return to the cave. The world was square, now; the paintings seemed even stranger, seen from Reed-Face's eyes. But she felt protected.

The walls began to speak to her slowly, catching her eye with paintings repeated over and over. The stories they told drifted into her thoughts. *Now there was a great rainstorm, and the river flooded. A boat full of fishermen is sinking. Twelve moons in a row. A new year. The great Fish-Man is dead. His mask is taken off, and put on the new Fish-Man. The Fish-Man marries the Sun-Woman. There is a big feast, and everyone is wearing masks that smile. A new year. The Sun-Woman has a sun-child. A girl. Here a boy enters a black hole. A cave full of terrifying things. Is it a dream-cave? He passes through. When he comes out, he carves a mask. Now he has a new face. Now the painter is painting himself painting. Did he run out of things to say? Or did he want to say, "I am the painter?" Another year . . . the Moon-*

Flash. She stopped in surprise, for there seemed to be many moon-flashes, all at once, circles with fire in them. Stick-figures were doing a confusing dance among the Moon-Flashes. Then the dance became clear, and her blood ran cold.

People are killing people.

"Terje," she whispered and began to run again.

The history faded into a colorful jumble around her. She ran past years, not knowing if she were going toward the beginning or the end of the story on the walls. The bone rattle shook a warning at her, but she paid no attention until, running finally out of history into daylight, she found herself surrounded by masks.

She stopped, panting. They all stared at each other: reed-faces, mud-faces, wood-faces, feather-faces. They had been waiting for her. Impulsively, she crouched, shook the bones at them to frighten them away.

They laughed and, murmuring among themselves, turned away from her to follow a trail down the cliff-side. *I am still Reed-Face*, she thought surprisedly Then she saw Terje.

She recognized his hands, paler than hers or any of the marked figures'. He wore a face carved out of wood, with a terrible scowl on it. She wanted to laugh at such a fierce mask on Terje's face, and she realized then how frightened she was. They were together again, close enough to touch each other, but she couldn't speak to him. He, too, was cloaked in fur, but his hands gathered the fur, closed in front of him, and his shoulders were hunched as though he were still cold. He didn't know her behind her mask. *Maybe*, she thought, *if I get close enough to him, we can run*. But all the mask-people merged into a single line, then, with Terje near the front. They began walking on a trail along the cliff that sloped gently toward the River, and Kyreol could do nothing but follow.

She saw boats moored in the distance and cheered up slightly. *We can steal a boat and sail away . . .* They were odd-looking boats, like little quarter-moons in the water. In the distance, she began to hear drums.

For some reason they frightened her more than anything else. Their voices were deep, hard, fast. A reed-face turned to a mud-face then and said something. Kyreol realized for the first time that, like birds, they spoke a different language.

Even her bones felt cold, then. She wondered if the River had tossed them into an entirely different world, if it were a path between two points in the sky, or between two dreams. *How can I say my name?* she thought, panicked. *That I am Kyreol of River-Tree and Turtle-Crossing, a safe place where people don't wear masks or steal each other away?*

Fortunately, no one said anything to her. The trail ended on a sandy shore where the boats were moored. They all clambered into the boats, their big masks bumping together as they knelt down. They faced downriver, and Kyreol wondered if they scared the fish. She watched the dip and circle of oars as they sped through the water toward the deep, violent voices of the drums. In a boat ahead, Terje sat still, his head bent. She wondered what he was thinking.

The boats angled across the river. The dark cliffs rose higher, towering against the sky. They changed as Kyreol looked at them. One moment they were simply stone walls bordering the river, with odd patterns of ridges and holes in them. The next moment, the patterns turned into stairs, walkways, doors, windows, carved into the rock. *They live in the cliffs*, Kyreol thought, and remembered the painting of the cliff-dwelling inside the caves.

More masks met them as they got out of the boats. The drums roared in triumph, then stopped abruptly. The crowd waiting on the shore parted, and a sun-mask walked through them.

The mask was a huge, round disk woven of reeds, then painted gold. The Sun had round eyes and a round mouth, and cheeks painted with green growing things. The masks from the boats greeted the Sun, and a woman's voice spoke in answer. Terje was brought forward. They took off his mask, so Kyreol could see his dirty, startled face. The Sun-Woman touched his hair. Then she took off her own mask.

Her hair was fair as Terje's. The crowd murmured behind her. The drums sounded again, softly. The woman said something to Terje. He shook his head a little. She snapped her fingers, and people from the crowd moved forward.

They took his fur cloak off, replaced it with a long cloak of tanned hide, painted with a swirl of masks and bodies. They put a spear in one of his hands and a bone knife in the other. When they began painting a moon-flash on his face with dye from a bowl the color of blood, something deep inside Kyreol that responded without words to dreams and the world lurched her whole body forward a step.

The Sun-Woman glanced absently toward the movement. Since she had already taken one step, Kyreol took another. Then another. Reed-Face moved strangely, jerkily toward Sun-Face, who had begun to frown. The bone rattle in Kyreol's hand dropped to her feet. She moved close enough to smell the various herbs that hung in little pouches from the Sun-Woman's cloak—herbs her father used. The Sun-Woman's face was painted sky-blue, with the blood red moon at moon-flash on one cheek and a ring of stars at the other. In the sudden silence, her voice curled upward in a question. Trembling, Kyreol removed the reed mask from her face.

Both Terje and the Sun-Woman stared at her. Before either of them could speak, Kyreol knelt down in the sand. She drew rapidly, without stopping to think. The River-sign. The sign for River-Tree and for Turtle-Crossing. She drew jagged lines for Fourteen Falls, with the rainbows arched over them, and the Sun-Woman made a soft noise. She drew the Moon-Flash and the Face beneath it, and then, in memory of her betrothal ritual, she laid her hand flat in the sand and made her handprint. She stopped a moment and realized that the jumble of pictures made no sense. So she began drawing again, more slowly.

This is the Face. This is the River. This is the boat with Terje and me in it, going toward the Falls. This is the boat, breaking in half, with two tiny people falling out of it. This is the cave where I slept. She drew a square face with square eyes over the sleeper The cave where the mask-people came.

The woman squatted and stopped her hand then.

She tapped at Reed-Face several times, saying a word over and over, until Kyreol understood what she wanted.

Where is Reed-Face?

She turned, pointed up the river, and the Sun-Woman nodded shortly. Then she looked at Kyreol for a long time out of her shrewd, wrinkled eyes. She snapped her fingers again, speaking, and two mud-masks came forward with bowls and began to paint Kyreol's face blue.

She and Terje huddled together later in a vast, firelit cave full of paintings of dreams and nightmares. They were alone; the cave entrances were guarded. Kyreol was surrounded by pots and bowls of paint, and Terje by weapons, drums, fierce masks, and round red shields with the flash of light hurtling into them.

Terje, scowling back at the masks, only answered Kyreol's questions in grunts until Kyreol asked in wonder, "Terje, did you forget your own language?"

He stirred. "No." His frown moved from the mask to her. But he wasn't seeing her. "They made me— They were waiting for me just outside the cave. They scared me. I tried to run, but they caught my arms and all the berries scattered all over the cave. I didn't understand for a while that the masks weren't their real faces. It was raining; night was coming; it was hard to see. They came out of the shadows like bad dreams . . . Then they put a face on my face, and I knew they were people. Like us. Only . . ." He paused, drawing breath. He let his head drop back against one of the dreams on the wall. "They took me to another cave. They kept touching my hair, looking into my face. I think they think I'm a ghost. They kept trying to teach me to throw a spear. At a mask and a bunch of twigs. Maybe they needed a hunter. Only the mask was a man's skull." He touched a spear point. "They kill each other."

"I know."

"Well, why?"

"I don't know."

His brows pinched together. "I can't think of any reason. How could people on the River come to be so different from us?"

"They have signs. They have a dream-cave. They know the Moon-Flash. Only here it doesn't mean good fortune or betrothal. It means—"

"Killing."

"That's so strange," she breathed. "The Moon-Flash has nothing to do with that. Everyone knows what it means."

"Maybe they're younger than we are. Their world hasn't been on the River as long as the Riverworld. So they make mistakes."

"Maybe," she said doubtfully. "Terje, how can people see and dream the same things, yet have a different language for them?"

He shook his head. "I don't know. Kyreol, let's go home."

"You dream." She sighed. "And then you tell me your dream bcause nobody else can understand you, and I paint it on the wall. Then they'll let us out. This isn't the world I wanted to find. I wanted the Hunter's world. He knows everything."

"How do they expect me to dream here? I can't sleep."

"Terje, this morning, just before I woke, I had a dream warning me of danger. Then I woke, and the mask-people found me."

"You dreamed—"

"Of the Hunter."

"The Hunter." He gazed silently at the full red moon of a shield. Then he said softly, "Well. Paint that on the wall. Then we can leave."

She lifted her head, smiling. So, on the inner walls of the dream-cave, among the frightening masks and animals and death-dreams, she painted a tall dark man cloaked in feathers, with the speaking crystal in his hand. She grew absorbed in her work, coloring the feathers neatly and accurately, so absorbed that she didn't hear Terje's sudden gasp, or see him rise and stumble against the weapons. When she turned finally, satisfied, she found two people watching her.

She whispered, when she could find her voice, "I painted you, and you came."

6

THE HUNTER had cloaked his feathers in fur. A wooden mask dangled by its strap from his hand. He was staring at the painting with a peculiar expression on his face, as if, Kyreol thought, he were seeing a turtle fly, or a boat sitting in a tree. He looked at Kyreol finally, with the same expression.

"What are you doing?"

"Well," she said shyly. "Terje couldn't dream. This is a dream-cave. So I painted my dream about you."

"Me."

"I dreamed you were trying to find me."

"I was," he said. "But how do you know what this place is?"

"I saw it in the paintings. The young boy enters the dark cave . . . He sees frightening things, or dreams a terrible dream. When he comes out, he makes his mask. Maybe Terje was supposed to dream his mask-face. But he couldn't, so I painted you. So we could leave."

The Hunter's mouth eased into a faint smile. "I see. Kyreol, I thought you and Terje must have died going over Fourteen Falls. I found the broken pieces of your boat. But here you are, deep in the sacred caves of another world, painting my face on the wall."

"You followed us," Terje said. He was back against a ferocious nightmare; his face seemed calm but wary.

"Yes."

"So you're not—you're not of the Riverworld."

"No."

"Or of this place."

"No."

"Oh." His shoulders eased a little against the stones. "How—why can we understand you? I couldn't understand the Sun-Woman."

"The world is full of languages." He contemplated Terje a moment, his face motionless as a mask. "Kyreol was the one who found me. Who asked the questions. What are you doing here?"

The side of Terje's mouth curved upward. "I just wanted to see the rainbows."

"Is that all?"

"Kyreol . . . she tells me stories, and then they come true. I had to come with her. Besides, the boat was ours together, and she needed it. And—"

"And?"

"She—we were always together, until she got betrothed. I didn't want her to go off by herself."

"I see."

"She wanted to find the end of the world. But it hasn't come to an end yet, and she won't go home."

"Even now?"

"Ask her."

"I want to see your world," Kyreol said patiently to the Hunter. "You know all the answers."

Th Hunter smiled, the dark, grave lines in his face softening. "You," he said, "are going to get me into trouble." He took out his crystal; it sprang open in his hand. "Channel two," he said softly. "Regny Orcrow. North Outstation Five. Acknowledge. Acknowledge."

"Acknowledged," the stone said. "Orcrow, where are you? Did you find the children?"

"Yes."

"Are you coming in? You missed the pickup craft; there won't be another here for two weeks."

"I know."

"Well, where are you?"

"I'm in the Cliff-Dwellers Passage of Dreams."

"You're . . . What on earth are you doing there? Are you hurt? In disguise? Do you want assistance? Where are the children?"

"Right here in front of me."

The stone's voice rose. "Orcrow, you're fired!"

The Hunter's mouth crooked ruefully. "Probably. But listen, it's a bit complicated—"

The stone didn't listen. It spoke steadily, angrily. The Hunter listened impassively, his eyes focussed on a distant point, as though he were watching an animal move slowly toward him. Finally he broke into the torrent of words. "All right. All right. I know. Ultimately I'm responsible. So right now, it's more important for me to get these two out of here than listen to you chew my ear off. Send a message to Domecity for me, will you? This might take longer than—"

"Orcrow! Take the kids back home and get to Outstation Five immediately. I'll request a pickup craft. Is that clear? Orcrow? Acknowledge—"

"Just send the message," Orcrow said. "I won't let any harm come to the children. Out." He closed the stone and sighed slowly. Then his head turned, with a hunter's alertness, toward some sound. He breathed, "Come."

He led them through a small passage in a wall of dreams and then upward, endlessly upward. The shining stone lit their way. Kyreol realized finally that they were travelling through the heart of the stone cliff, behind the dwellings. The Hunter did not let them speak, but they met no one in the damp, winding pathway. Finally, they reached what seemed must be the top of the world.

It was night. The sky was a glittering cap of stars touching all horizons. The vast circle of blackness rising up to meet the stars was the world as Kyreol had never seen it. She shivered in the wind, not with cold, but with wonder, and she wanted to peel back the blackness to see what marvels lay around them.

"Where is your home?" she asked the Hunter, and his answer stretched the world even farther.

"At the end of the River. You can't see it from here." He added mysteriously, "The world curves."

"Will you take us there?"

He was silent for a long time. His face was motionless against the brilliant stars, as though it were carved out of river stone. "Not yet," he said finally. "I have to leave you."

"But—"

"Can you sail in the dark?"

"Yes," Terje said gruffly.

"I'll show you a trail back down to the river. There will be a boat tied there. Take it, and go swiftly. As swiftly as you can. Don't sleep. You'll hear drums; you'll see fires. Don't stop. Keep to the middle of the river. If you see any other boats, try to hide until they pass. And, here—" He gave Kyreol his stone. "This is for good luck. If you are in danger, open it and speak to it."

She took it from him, feeling cold again as the shining slid into her fingers. "My mother's stone," she whispered. "The dream-stone."

"Go downriver until dawn. Then, if you want to go home, open the stone and tell it that. Someone will come to lead you back." He put his hands on their shoulders, led them across the top of the cliff to a trail. "Hurry."

"But, wait—" Kyreol cried, standing still against his hold, and she saw him smile a little. "Will we see you again?"

"I don't know. But I think so." His hands nudged them forward. "Go." He put on his mask, then; the last glimpse Kyreol had of him was a black oval face with white circles widening on it, like ripples on the river. Then the mask turned away from them, and he was gone.

The high cliffs blotted out the stars until they were once again a thin, curving river of light far above, mirroring the path of the water. The small boat tugged against its moorings at the trail's end. The Hunter had put food in it, fishing lines, a tiny lamp, his knife, and Terje sighed with relief. They pushed the boat out and spent a few moments turning circles until they learned to handle the oars. Then, catching the

67

swift current, they rowed, out of the place of masks and caves and harshly singing drums, into morning.

At sunrise, they stared at each other, their faces smudgy with sleeplessness. The cliffs were gone. The river had broadened and flowed slowly through groves of odd trees with prickly, honey-colored barks and plump, yellow fruit. The banks were sandy gold. The blue sky seemed to have no beginning and no end.

They pulled the boat up onto the sand and lay in the warm light, their faces turned toward the sun like flowers. They ate dried fish and cracked nuts lazily, tossing shells into the river. The water was so clear they could see the stippled backs of fishes flickering through the gold-green depths. The sun climbed higher into the sky; distant mists dispersed, and the river glinted toward a far, flat horizon.

Terje counted days and nights on his fingers. "Two —three—four. This is the fourth day we've been gone. Kyreol, your father must be worried."

"I'll send him a dream," Kyreol said drowsily, "so he'll know I'm coming back."

"We should go back now. Open the stone and tell it."

"No . . ." she pleaded. "Just a little farther. Besides . . ." The river dimpled and tugged at her words. "You want to be back for Moon-Flash. For your betrothal. I'll have to go back to Korre. I won't see you anymore, then. Now, I have you with me for a while. Like we used to be."

He rolled over, his back to the sun. She looked at him, but he wasn't looking at her, he was frowning at the distance. The strange, spikey leaves of the trees rattled drily in the breeze. Then his eyes came to her face. He smiled, the leaf-shadows sliding over his hair and his bare arms.

"They'll be angry with us."

"But when we're old—old as that man in Little Spring—we can tell each other stories of going to the end of the world. And everyone else will think we dreamed it. But we'll know."

"This place is beautiful," he said softly. "If there are people here, I wonder how they dream."

She picked up the stone, which she had laid carefully beside the dried fish. It dazzled in her fingers. She turned it, pressed facet after facet, murmuring, "How can I get inside you, dream-stone? I want to talk to you." It opened itself to her finally. It's insides, delicate threads of crystal and gold, made no sense to her. She held it in her palm as she had seen the Hunter do. "Stone, this is Kyreol. I am talking to you from the place beyond the cliff dwellings, where there are big yellow trees and the river is peaceful."

There was a flurry of strange language within the stone. She blinked. Terje leaned forward to listen. "Stone. I can't understand you."

A different voice spoke; the language became comprehensible. "Who are you?"

"It's me. Kyreol. Of River-Tree and Turtle-Crossing."

"Kyreol—"

"The Hunter gave me this stone. Orcrow," she added carefully, and the stone said a word she didn't understand.

"Where is he?"

"I don't know. He went away. Terje is here, though."

"Listen," the stone said. "Listen to me carefully. Tell me exactly where you are, then stay there. Don't move. Someone will come and lead you back to—"

"But we don't want to go back," Kyreol said patiently. "Not yet. I like seeing new places. I just wanted to talk to you, tell you what I'm seeing."

The stone was silent a moment. "What are you seeing? Exactly?"

She looked up, preparing to describe the sky and the trees. But Terje shifted abruptly, put a finger on his lips. So she said, "Stone, I have to go now. Goodbye." She pressed it closed. Terje had already risen and was pushing the boat into the water. She gathered their food reluctantly.

"I want to sleep. Then I want to swim."

"Later." He stopped moving and straightened, gazing at the huge blank sky, the golden land, and he laughed suddenly, as if he had just glimpsed their freedom. They splashed through the shallows, skimming the boat with them, then hoisted themselves into it and rowed, while behind them a startled flock of yellow birds swept like a shower of leaves out of the trees.

For a long while then they lost track of time. They let the river carry them through changeless days and starry nights. They slept on soft banks beneath their fur; they swam and fished and tasted strange fruit and counted the number of birds they had never seen before. They made pipes out of reeds and played them when they ran out of stories to tell. The Riverworld seemed as far away as the moon, and they left no traces of themselves along the river for anyone to follow.

One night the breeze brought them a faint scent of

smoke and roast fish that seemed to come from nowhere. In the morning, they searched the banks cau-
tiously, but saw nothing, not even charred wood.
Later that day as they sailed in a lazy silence, they
heard what might have been a light flurry of tiny
bells. They watched the shores sharply, but saw no
one, until dusk, when a shadow in the sand seemed to
detach itself from the twilight and move deeper into
the night.

"It might be an animal," Terje said.

"Animals don't cook fish. They don't wear bells."

"We thought we smelled fish. We thought we
heard bells."

"People don't think they hear bells in the middle
of a desert. Either they do or they don't," Kyreol said.
She was cross because she was afraid. But Terje only
laughed, guiding the boat into shallows on the other
side of the river. Maybe his laughter was reassuring
to their shadow, for that night they saw a single flame
on the shore across from them. The next morning they
saw nothing at all. But at midmorning, as the sun
peeled away the last of the night coolness and the
river burned as brightly as the sky, they saw a figure
striding across the sand dunes along the bank, keeping
abreast of their boat.

It vanished after a while, slipped in the wink of
an eye back into the desert. But not before they heard
again the teasing shake of bells.

As they sat at their own fire at dusk, eating fruit and
fish, a boy appeared out of the wind in front of them.
He had settled himself cross-legged and laid a strange
ball in front of Terje, before Kyreol, her mouth hanging open, realized that he hadn't come out of the air.

There were his footprints in the sand. But he had walked so quietly, as quietly as a bird's wing brushing the evening.

"Who are you?" she breathed. But he only shook his head, smiling, and prodded his gift. Terje touched it puzzledly. It was big, round, hard as a nut and hairy.

"Maybe it's some kind of drum," Kyreol guessed, rapping it with her knuckles. She transferred her attention back to the boy. He was very tall, very thin, all bones and angles. His skin was dark, but not as dark as hers. He wore a length of black cloth tucked over one shoulder, under one arm, and draped down around his knees. The cloth looped up again, wound around his hips a few times, then was tucked back into itself to make a pocket. His eyes were very dark, his hair dark and curly; his smile was wide and very friendly. He stopped smiling briefly, to gaze back at them, and there was an imperious, watchful tilt to his face. Then his teeth flashed cheerfully, and he unfolded his bony fingers, pushed at the ball again.

"It's a game," Terje guessed.

"Where does he keep his bells?"

Terje picked up the ball. He sniffed at it suddenly, then shook it. The boy laughed and held out his hand for it. In the firelight, pictures danced on the underside of his arm, telling a story from his wrist to his shoulder.

He saw them staring and promptly pulled the cloth down around his waist. The story marched across his chest in vivid colors and odd shapes and then back down his other arm.

Kyreol stared, fascinated. There were birds in the story, strange signs, bright lines of dots, intricate knots of color. The boy's smile disappeared again; he gazed with pride at his arms. Then he reached across the fire, touched Terje's bare, upturned arm.

The lack of pictures on it seemed to bewilder him. He tapped Terje's wrist a few times, his eyes demanding an answer to his puzzlement. Kyreol giggled at the image of a painted Terje.

"He has as many signs on him as the betrothal carpet. Look, Terje, there's a butterfly. And two snakes. Maybe it's just . . ."

"Just what?"

"I don't know." She brushed a flat space in the sand and drew their own signs. "This is me. A tree and a turtle. And this is Terje. Three Rocks." She added, "That's all we have." She touched her forehead. "We paint them there."

The smile shone again; the boy nodded approvingly. He tapped his left wrist and then his heart and then his wrist again. He held his arm above the fire for them to see his sign.

A white circle, a star of fire . . . Kyreol's voice went small with astonishment. "Moon-Flash."

The boy's head lifted. The moon was only a thin curve of white in the sky, but he stretched out his arm toward it, showing his sign, in a movement that was at once a ritual and a proud gesture of kinship. Watching his face, Kyreol thought, *The moon recognizes him. He is the moon's child. The son of a healer, maybe, or a ruler, like the Sun-Woman.*

"But where is his home?" she asked aloud. "And where are his bells?" She tilted her head, shook something invisible near her ear. "Bells." She tapped her ear, then pointed at the boy and tinkled the invisible

73

bells again. The third time she did it, the intent look left his face, and he laughed.

He untucked the end of his cloth and spread it flat on the sand. Kyreol, gazing at the small collection of possessions, realized that he had nothing else. He had his sandals, the voluminous length of cloth, the vast blue sky, and the endless sand. He separated things carefully, laying them out on the cloth, his long fingers gesturing, talking. A stone for fire. A tiny net of leather laces attached to a bone handle. He demonstrated that, sending a stone hurtling out of the net into the night. A small knife with the most beautiful handle Kyreol had ever seen. Bells. He had wound cloth tightly around them to keep them silent. He shook them into his palm: tiny bells stitched to circlets of leather. He slid them over his wrists and shook them, smiling at their expressions. A few bundles of dried herbs. A small skin for water. That was all.

Terje drew a breath. "He's all alone in the desert, taking care of himself."

"Maybe he's learning to be a hunter."

"Maybe. But he doesn't have a spear or arrows, or traplines. Not even fishing line . . ."

She watched the fearless, eager eyes flicking back and forth as they talked, as he listened for one familiar word. But he seemed patient with his wordlessness, as though their language was just one more noise among all the vast and varied noises made on the earth. He caught her eye, and the ready smile sprang forth again. She smiled back.

"Maybe," she said, "he's just learning to live." She drew houses in the sand, little people, and finally he grunted. He gestured away from the river. His people lived that way, under the rising sun. He raised his arm again, showed his sign to the moon, then swept his hand around him, circling the desert. Then he tapped the moon on his wrist, and then his heart.

They shook their heads over that one. He grinned, and raising the ball he had given Terje, he cracked it in two like an egg against a stone.

"It's something to eat!" Kyreol said. He handed them the dripping halves, and they drank a sweet, milky liquid. He showed them how to pry the thick white flesh from its shell. They offered him fish in return, but he shook his head, munching at the fruit. Then he made a small face, and they laughed. Fish, his expression said. Nothing to eat but fish.

Then he was gone. A shadow, a brush of wind, leaving not even a name they could call. A boy, kin to the moon, learning how to live under the sun.

"I wonder what his dreams are like," Kyreol murmured later as they lay beside the embers, listening to the river sigh. "Terje."

He grunted.

"We never even spoke. Terje . . ."

"What?"

"That was a different Moon-Flash. How many things can Moon-Flash mean?" She didn't hear if he answered; she was drifting gently into her night journey. The thin moon-paring hovered before her in her dreaming, giving her no answers.

The land began to change, then. The silky desert sand bunched up into hard dry hills covered with stones and scrub brush. Far in the distance a mist slowly became a line of blue mountains, marching across the desert. Kyreol wondered what kinds of

75

people lived among the high jagged peaks. They began to be wakened by odd noises in the dead of nights. One morning, their boat curved around a bend in the river and interrupted a herd of animals, big as small huts, lumbering into the water to drink.

Kyreol groped urgently for the stone, which she had all but forgotten, while Terje, his muscles hard with exertion, sped to the far side of the river.

"Stone. This is Kyreol." She spoke softly, so as not to annoy the animals. But they seemed more interested in blowing water out of their noses at each other. "Stone."

"Kyreol!" the stone shouted.

"Sh!"

"You're still alive!"

"Stone, there are some enormous animals in the river—they're grey and black, and they have teeth as long as this boat sticking out of their mouths."

"Stay away from them."

"Oh, we will." Her mouth was dry. "Will they stay away from us?"

"I hope so."

"Stone, what are they?"

The stone hesitated. "Animals," it said finally.

"Well, I know that, but—" A blaze of color caught her eye. "Now there is a cloud of birds. Green, with white stripes down their wings. As tall as people." She listened, entranced as one of them sang. It was a haunting song, deep and pure as notes out of a huge reed pipe. "Stone—"

"I hear it."

"Where are we? Is this the same world?"

The stone seemed to sigh. It spoke to itself a moment, quickly, incomprehensibly. Then it said carefully, "There are places in the world where animals are gathered to live freely, away from people. You're passing through one of them. Kyreol—"

"What language were you speaking?" she asked abruptly. "Is it the Hunter's language?"

"It—yes."

"Will you teach it to me?"

There was another conversation within the stone, much longer than before. Then it said resignedly to her, "Wouldn't you rather go home?"

"No."

"Then—all right. At least I'll know you're still alive. Now listen carefully." It said something slowly. "That means, 'My name is Joran.' Now say this."

She repeated it delightedly. "My name is Kyreol. Terje, listen!" She caught his arm, making the boat swerve. "You say this: 'My name is Terje.' "

He pulled up his oar, looking in disbelief at an enormous, silky animal with a mane sunning itself on the shore and then at her. "My name is Terje," he said huskily. "Now ask it what that is."

They spoke to the stone intermittently throughout the day, learning the names of dozens of birds and animals, along with the words for boat, fish, fire, tired, hungry, river, world. Only when Kyreol asked the word for Moon-Flash did the stone refuse her.

"You'll have to ask the Hunter."

The stone advised that they stay in the boat, so they rarely left it. They kept it in mid-river, taking turns sleeping at night while the other rowed. During the day, in clearings where they saw no animals, they stopped briefly to cook the fish they caught, to gather fruit that Joran told them was safe to eat.

One night Kyreol, lulled to sleep by the water eddying in moonlit circles away from the lift and dip of Terje's oar, had a dream. It was so quick that she seemed to dream it between closing and opening her eyes. One moment she saw the night with its great herd of stars; the next she saw the Hunter, handing her father a stone, and then she saw the stars again, and Terje's back. The stone in the dream had had three River-signs on it: River-Tree, Turtle-Crossing, Green Pool. Her father, taking the stone from the Hunter, had looked at the signs and nodded. She woke and sat silently for a few moments, listening to a night-bird cry.

"Green Pool . . ."

Terje half-turned. "What?"

"Your sign is Three Rocks. Why would I dream about Green Pool?"

Terje was silent for three dips of the oar. "It's your mother's family," he said gruffly. "What did you dream?"

Kyreol sat up, rocking the boat. "It's all right, then," she said in relief.

"What is?"

"They all came together—the Hunter, my father, my sign, my mother's sign—all in the same dream. The Hunter gave my father some kind of message. So he understands, a little."

Terje grunted. His shoulders were a strong, pale line against the stars, moving steadily, effortlessly. "Go to sleep," he said haltingly, in the new language they were learning. "Dream. Dream tomorrow."

Kyreol closed her eyes.

7

SHE WOKE UP at dawn, when Terje stopped the boat. The river was flat grey, and so slow the boat barely drifted when he raised the oars. He held them suspended like wings while he stared at the banks. She lifted her head. The land was harsh, treeless; nothing moved around them but thin mists, uncoiling and wisping away from the great stone faces that were watching them.

Kyreol felt a finger of cold run up and down her spine. She moved forward, pushing herself against Terje's back for comfort.

"What are they?" she whispered.

The faces were scattered all over the banks. They were black, elongated, with big, distant eyes under frowning brows, and full, straight mouths. They looked taller than houses. Stone giants, who had been buried to their necks in the earth, and then forgotten.

She felt Terje draw a soft breath. "They don't want us here," he said, trying to figure out what story they were telling. He was right, Kyreol felt; they made her want to leave quickly.

"But what are they guarding? There's nothing here." She was still whispering, as though the stone ears could hear. "Terje, they don't look angry. Not like the mask-faces. They look . . ." What did they look? Cold, lonely, fierce, stuck in dead earth beside the still river . . . Sad?

"Ask the stone."

But the stone didn't answer; maybe it was still asleep. "Joran," Kyreol said, correcting herself. "Joran is asleep." Stones didn't speak, not even this one. But stone faces seemed to speak, in a language far simpler than words. She wanted Terje to row again, quickly, but before she could say that, she heard her mouth say, "I want to go look at them."

Terje turned around. His mouth was open; he closed it, a mute stubbornness spreading over his face. "I don't."

"But, Terje—"

"Kyreol, you can hear what the faces are saying. There must be a reason why they're telling us to stay away. I don't want to find out what." She drew breath; he gestured, almost losing the oars. "First we almost kill ourselves going down Fourteen Falls. Then we get captured by mask-people. Then we have to learn another language from someone who talks into a stone, when one language is enough for any world— Kyreol, what are you looking for? What is it you want to know? How much farther do you want to go?"

"I don't know," she said. She drew away from him. "I want to do what I want to do. You're just afraid of missing your betrothal."

"Kyreol, that doesn't have anything to do with it!"

"They're just old stones; they can't hurt us."

"They're not just stones. They're part of somebody's ritual. Would you want strangers wandering around in the betrothal caves?"

She pointed, east and west. "Look. Do you see anyone?"

He angled the oars into the boat with a clatter. "But why?" he demanded, bewildered and angry. "Why?"

She was silent. Water lapped against the sides of the boat. Three black birds flew over the greyness. She realized then how far she was taking them both, not only from home, but from a way of looking at the world. To Terje, the world beyond Fourteen Falls was difficult and interesting, but he would shed the knowledge of it as a bird sheds water when he went back home. There was something in him that did not want to be changed.

She looked away from his eyes. She scratched her head uncertainly, groping for words. The faces watched, silent, disturbing. "When I see—when I see things like this—or the mask-faces, the cave paintings, it's like seeing into people's dreams. Dreams say things without words. They talk about the world. I just want to know why—what people saw to make them build faces like those." She paused, felt him waiting. "Terje," she said helplessly. "I didn't know the world would be this big, beyond Fourteen Falls. I thought it would be simpler. I don't know how much more of it there is. But it keeps going on, and I keep wanting to see where it goes."

She raised her eyes finally to his face. He sat very quietly; she was aware, suddenly, of a quietness that always seemed to be with him, even when he was shouting down the rapids toward the rainbows, or sitting in the dream-cave with a spear in front of him. He was like the Riverworld, peaceful and unafraid. Except when she disturbed him. He made her feel noisy, impulsive, always wanting things without reason, like a child. *Look at this, Terje—look at that, Terje.* And suddenly she was looking at Terje and seeing for the first time not the child he had been but what he had become.

She couldn't speak any more. Somehow they had become two different people. She was sitting in a boat in the middle of a world with a stranger. She felt blood rise into her face and was glad he couldn't see it. He needed to go home; he needed to become betrothed, take his place as a man in the Riverworld.

"All right," she whispered. She would do that for him: take him home, because he wouldn't leave her.

"All right, what?" His voice sounded strange. His eyes seemed as opaque as the water.

"Terje. Let me just look at the faces. And then we'll go home."

"All right." But he couldn't seem to move. She wondered if he even knew what she had said.

"Terje—"

"Kyreol—"

They both stopped. Then they were both smiling, and his face was familiar again. He lifted the oars as though he had forgotten what he had been arguing about and rowed toward the silent bank.

The faces loomed over them as they moored the boat. They seemed gigantic, eerie, full of secrets locked within the stone. They rose like trees in a treeless field, like questions out of the ground. She stood in front of one, gazed up at it. It was too big for her to see its full expression. Its mouth turned downward; harsh furrows ran down its cheeks. It seemed to hold not anger, but a terrible silence inside itself. She circled it slowly.

The back of the head was flat and carved with signs. Kyreol traced them with her finger. "The story," she whispered. "A man . . . three little men . . ."

"Children?"

"Children. Three children? Three animals . . . the children turned into animals?"

"That doesn't make sense."

"Terje, everything in the world doesn't have to— Oh—" Her voice faltered. "Now the children are inside the animals. Terje, I think they got eaten. The man is crying. Look at the big tears falling down. Now he has a spear, and he's following the animals . . . Now . . ." she touched a circle with a tiny lightning bolt entering it. "Now . . ." Her fingers traced the rim of the circle, then the bolt of fire. "Moon-Flash," she said surprisedly, and the back of the face sprang open. A skeleton rattled slowly to its knees, then broke to pieces at their feet.

They were back in the boat so quickly that Kyreol couldn't remember getting her feet wet. She sat gripping the sides of the boat, her eyes enormous, while Terje spun circles in the shallows. She closed her eyes tightly. They were trapped, they would never get out. The boat lurched forward, skimmed across the water.

"I told you," she heard Terje say from a distance. "I told you."

Her voice squeaked, "Just go." After a while, she let go of the sides of the boat. She wanted to huddle at the bottom of it, hide until the faces were far behind. "I'm sorry," she whispered, both to Terje and the bones she had disturbed. "I'm sorry." She opened her eyes finally and saw trees.

Terje's rowing slowed. He upended the oars finally, sat panting. His face was a peculiar color, and she remembered he had rowed most of the night. He didn't say anything. She wondered if he would ever forgive her.

"Terje," she said tentatively. He looked at her, not seeing her.

"It's not right," he whispered. He looked drunk, his face patchy-white and wild-eyed with some idea. She reached for the oars, wondering uneasily if the bones had become a nightmare in his mind.

"I'll row."

"No."

"Terje—I'm sorry—"

"It's not right." He grabbed the oars suddenly and steered toward the trees. "You stay. I'll go."

Her voice wavered. "Are you going home?"

"No," he said impatiently. "I'm going to put the bones back."

Her own bones felt heavy as stones. She wanted to melt like a puddle into the bottom of the boat. "Oh, please," she breathed. "Oh, please don't. Terje, please—"

"It's not right to leave them there."

"Oh, please." The boat bumped against the bank. "Wait here."

"Terje."

He glared at her suddenly, scared and furious.

"You don't disturb things in other people's places. Especially not the dead. How can we just leave him there?" He tossed her fur onto the bank. "He'll get rained on—Kyreol, if you don't get out of the boat, I'll take you with me."

She stumbled out, her feet sinking into muddy water. She stood watching as he rowed away, without a glance at her, until he disappeared around the trees. And then her legs shook so much, she had to sit.

It was an endless wait. The leaves sighed. Fish jumped in front of her. The sun came out, drawing the grey out of the water. But Terje didn't come. He had been taken by ghosts, he had died of terror, something had eaten him . . . She sat still as a statue, scarcely daring to breath. Her thoughts grew quieter, finally, as the sun warmed her. She thought of the man who had lost his children and then his life. Maybe the stone face protecting him was the most peaceful place he had ever known. Certainly the world itself wasn't very peaceful. And then she thought of the Moon-Flash. And then of Terje.

He came back finally, his face still looking peculiar, but more peaceful. He smiled a little when he saw her, and she went to meet him. She wanted to put her arms around him; but he had been among the dead by choice, and she felt suddenly too shy to touch him. He sat down on the bank. She sat beside him, and he moved closer, put his arm around her, wanting something living to touch.

She shifted after a while, drawing breath. "Terje."

"What?"

"The Moon-Flash. It means—it means something

85

else here." She paused, remembering. "I touched it, and the stone opened and the bones came out. It means death."

"Kyreol, it was hard getting the bones back in. They kept sliding out." He looked at her, the color struggling back into his face. "That's a sad way to die. No one dies like that in the Riverworld."

She said reluctantly, "I promised to go back with you now."

"You did? When?"

"When we were arguing. You—" Her eyes faltered away from his eyes. "Don't you remember? You need to go home."

He was silent, frowning puzzledly, not at her, but at something in himself. "I was never so scared in my life," he confessed. "My hair should be white, like an old man's. But I don't think—I don't want to go home now. Not yet."

"But—"

"There's nothing all that different from the River-world. People live and die and dream dreams. It's still all one world." He was silent again, then he looked straight at her, holding her eyes before she could turn away. "What will you do?" he asked calmly. "Go back to Turtle-Crossing and listen to Korre talk about fishing?"

Her shoulders wriggled under his hold. "Well," she said irritably, "you won't go home by yourself. And you have to go home."

"Why? I think I like being scared."

"Because—"

"Because why?"

"Because—"

86

"Why?"

"Because," she said, exasperated, "I used to be taller than you. And now you're taller than me. And I don't know what you're laughing about—if we were still children, it would be all right."

He stopped laughing. With the sun in his eyes, it was hard for her to tell what he was thinking. He stood up suddenly, pushed the boat back into the water and got in.

"Where are you going?" she called.

"Fishing." He read her thoughts, then, and tossed her the crystal before she asked for it.

"Terje—"

"Nothing has changed," he said calmly. "You just think it has."

She sat back down on the bank, bewildered. I've changed, she thought, and tried to hear the new blood flowing through her heart. But all she could hear were singing birds.

She opened the stone finally. "Joran," she said, and he answered. She made a weave of the two languages, too impatient to wait for him to translate. "This morning, we saw the faces beside the river."

"The faces?"

"The black stone faces with the dead inside them—"

"Kyreol," he shouted, and she drew back, wondering how such a delicate thing could hold so huge a shout. "How do you know about the dead?"

"It was an accident," she said in a small voice. "I touched a Moon-Flash, and the bones fell out. Terje put them back. What did you say?"

"Never mind. Go on."

"That's what I wanted to ask about. The Moon-

Flash. In the Riverworld, it is a sign for the living. Here, it is a sign for the dead. Which is it, really? The Moon-Flash?"

She heard the stone sigh. "If you go far enough," Joran said, "you'll find out. I can't tell you."

"But you know."

"I can't tell you, Kyreol. Child, how have you gotten so far down the river and survived? Do you have any idea who those graves belong to?"

"No."

"One of the fiercest river-tribes in the world. If they had caught you on their sacred ground, they would have killed you."

"Oh," she said without sound.

"Where are you now?"

"There was no one there. Among the dead."

"You were very lucky. Where are you?"

"Downriver, beside some trees. Terje is catching breakfast."

"Well, breakfast can wait. You get back in the boat and get out of there. You're probably out of danger now, but go anyway." She sighed. "And where is that blasted Orcrow? He'll be lucky if he finds a job recycling garbage after this."

"Stone," she interrupted. "Where in this world is there a safe place?"

"Home. Where you came from."

"Please—"

"Outside of stray animals, storms and the river itself, you'll be safe. For a while. Shall I send someone?"

"Soon, I think," she whspered. "But not yet."

She called Terje. He had caught a fish, but they didn't stop to cook it. Since he had been up most of the night, she rowed, and he slept until midday when they found a secluded clearing where they could build a fire. Then he rowed, while she cast out the lines, caught more fish for their supper. The river grew deep and swift, carrying them farther and farther from the place of the dead, until, by evening, it seemed to have swept them into yet another world of bare, rolling hills, small groves of twisted trees and birds that flamed like scraps of the sunset among the branches.

They stopped finally in the shadow of a hill. The river's voice, rattling through rock shallows, was a soothing sound. The world seemed peaceful again, uninhabited by dreams. They lay close to the fire after they had eaten, watching the little boat-moon sail among the star-fish.

"I'm getting tired of eating fish," Terje murmured, just before he drifted to sleep. Kyreol, closing her eyes, saw the dark, grieving faces rise once again out of a dank mist and shivered. She reached out, stirred the fire. Light touched her face like a hand, and she floated again downriver for a while, laughing, fishing, eating fruit yellow as sunlight. Then the faces again . . . the Moon-Flash . . .

She opened her eyes. Terje lay with his face toward the stars, one arm crooked around his head. The fire sparked, warming her again. She lifted her dark fingers, caught fire in them, then let them fall again, close to Terje's hand. Such a small distance between them . . . between touching and not touching, waking and sleeping. She raised her head a little, watched the light flow across his face, and something filled her like another set of bones within her bones, covered her like

8

THE NEXT MORNING, before she even opened her eyes, Kyreol tried to count the days until Moon-Flash. But she had lost track of the patterns of the moon, and the days on the river had flowed together like water. Even her body, startled by the long journey, had forgotten to respond to the moon-changes. She opened her eyes. A red sun rose slowly; birds began calling to it. The wind came out of the nameless desert, touched her face lightly. *Where are we?* she wondered. *We're in the middle of nowhere. No one came to name this place.* Terje stirred as the light touched his eyes. She watched him blink, coming back from the journey of his dreams. He turned his head after a moment, saw her awake and smiled.

His hand came out of the fur, closed over her fingers. She lay looking at him, dark and silent, until his hand rose, ran over her face softly, like the wind. She bent her head very slowly, a new movement, something her body had decided to do. Their lips touched lightly, like leaves.

She sat up again, feeling the blood rush into her face.

"Terje." Her voice sounded husky.

"What?"

"When is the Moon-Flash?"

He drew breath silently, loosed it just as silently. Then, abruptly, he rose. "I don't know. Ask the stone." He took two steps away from her, then knelt down beside her, held her arms. "Kyreol," he said softly, "I don't know what to do."

"Well," she said bleakly, her hands rising to his shoulders. His skin was warm, damp from sleep, his muscles hard from rowing. She swallowed. "I don't either," she whispered. "Maybe, if we are patient, the river will tell us."

He said nothing more. He waded into the water until it covered all of him like a skin, then he dove deep, surfaced farther away, dove deep again. Kyreol gathered wood, puzzling over the problem. She wanted Terje, wanted him with her always. She wanted to breathe the air that he breathed, dream the same dreams, grow so close to him that she wouldn't be able to remember whose face was whose. But there was Korre. And there was Jage. And if they did grow so close, she and Terje, there would be no place for them within the familiar life and rituals of the Riverworld.

Terje came back finally and took the boat out to fish. He was gone a long time. She searched the trees and bushes and found birds pecking at small red fruit on a tree. She picked one and tasted it. It was sweet, juicy, with a single pit inside. She climbed the tree and tossed handfuls down to the ground.

By the time she jumped down from the tree, she

felt better. *We can ask my father*, she thought. *He'll know what we should do.* She gathered the fruit. Terje had returned; he was whittling twigs to spit the fish on. His face looked calmer. She felt shy of him suddenly, unable to meet his eyes. But he sensed that. He laid aside his knife and stood up to kiss her cheek. When she looked at him finally, he was smiling, and they could talk again.

The world loomed in front of them, vast dangerous, and even more mysterious than before. They went on because it didn't seem time, yet, to go back. There were too many questions unanswered; they hadn't come to the Hunter's world, yet. The moon's eye closed and opened, alternately watching and dreaming. By day, the sky blazed above them, so taut and blue-white it might have been made of crystal. Once, twice, during the long journey, things disturbed it. Tiny things no bigger than insects, silver, red. Kyreol, lounging in the boat while Terje rowed, a big leaf over her head to shield her eyes from the sun, followed the flight of one of the glittering things. It left a gossamer scar across the sky like a spider's casting.

"Terje," she said, waving her leaf at it. "Is that thing very tiny or very big?"

Terje gazed upward. The oars stilled in his hands; the boat drifted. His mouth opened a little. "I don't know. Sometimes stars do that . . . but not so slowly."

"Well, are stars tiny or big?"

His mouth closed, curled upward. "How would I know? I don't know more than you do."

"Yes, you do."

"How could I?"

She nibbled on the leaf-edge, searching for words.

93

"For you, the world is one big piece, and all the little pieces you see already fit somewhere into your big piece. I just see the little pieces, all jumbled up, all different, with nothing making much sense."

"You're not making much sense."

"Now you sound like Korre." As soon as she said the name, she was sorry. Their eyes met; little questions passed between them. Will you go back to Korre? What will you do if I do? What will you do if I don't?

The river seemed to flow forever through a flat, gold land with no people and few animals. All days became the same day, peaceful, uneventful, until it seemed they had entered a timeless country; they were trapped in the endless boundary of the world. Only the growing collection of new words the stone taught them made one afternoon different from another. Then one day the river curled unexpectedly back into time, making them realize how far they had come from the Face.

Kyreol was rowing, looking ahead for the Hunter's world while Terje fished for dinner, his face toward the past. Kyreol, trying to stay awake under the glittering sun, watched the oar bend into a crooked line beneath the water and wondered why it did that. She watched their shadows lengthen slowly and wondered why people stayed at one height during the day, but their shadows grew constantly big and small. She watched a bird dive for a fish and wondered why the First Bird, who dwelt in the air, had decided to eat its First Fish, who lived in water. She made up a story about an argument between them that grew so heated the bird ate the fish to make it stop talking. It made Terje laugh. Then something she had been watching without thinking about for a long time began to grow bigger and become strange.

Ahead, the bare land wrinkled into small hills. There seemed to be a dust storm around them, but there was, she realized, no wind. Yet dust flew off them in little puffs. As she leaned forward, unconsciously putting more strength into her rowing, she saw something walk over one of the hills.

"Terje."

There were more movements. She stopped rowing suddenly and reached for the stone. Terje turned around.

"People," he said, surprised.

"Maybe it's another burial ground," Kyreol said nervously. She opened the crystal. "Joran."

"Kyreol," the stone said, and asked immediately, as always, "where are you?"

"Stone, there are some little hills in front of us. Dust is blowing across them, but there's no wind. And there are people. Is it dangerous? Are they burying their dead?"

The stone was silent. Kyreol waited, then peered into it, then shook it. "Stone—"

"I'm here. I can't believe you've made it so far already."

"Where are we?"

"Kyreol, I don't know what to do with you anymore."

"That's all right, Stone. I don't either. But what—Will we be safe?"

"Oh, yes. Very safe. Just row past the hills, and—"

"What are they?"

"You'll see a house. A big house made of sandstone.

Stop there. The man there will be able to answer your questions. Talk to me again when you get there."

"Whose house?"

"Don't worry. I'll let him know you're coming."

"All right." She paused, eyeing the fragile threads inside the crystal, and asked in spite of herself, "Joran, how do you do that?"

"What?"

"Put your voice into the stone." The stone sighed. "Also, we saw some little tiny things high in the sky. They flew—"

"Kyreol, I must go. Orcrow will explain everything. He'd better. Don't worry—"

"But where is he?" Kyreol asked. The stone didn't answer.

She sat back, frowning. "I don't know if I want to go inside a strange house. They might try to send us back."

Terje shrugged. The sun had baked his skin the color of the desert, giving him a dusty look. His hair was damp with sweat. "We can always run away again," he said wearily. "Kyreol, you'll have to get your answers from people, you can't do it by yourself. Besides, maybe they'll have something to eat besides fish."

"Nut bread," she said.

"Stuffed eggs."

"Turtle soup."

"Honey wine."

She handed him the oars. "Here. You row faster than I do."

As they rowed past the hills, men standing on the

top of them shaded their eyes with their hands as if they couldn't believe what they were seeing. Then they waved. Kyreol waved back shyly. The hills were there because the people were digging holes for some reason. They weren't sad, as at a funeral, and nothing of value that Kyreol could see went in or out of the holes. They were just people, some dark, some pale, dressed in plain, skimpy clothes, digging holes in a desert under the fiery sun.

"It makes no sense," Kyreol said.

The house was far more than a house. It was a huge high square with sandstone pillars beside the doors. Two half-circles of stone jutted out from its sides. Trees with delicate yellow flowers grew around the great house. The still river mirrored it, quiet and majestic against the blue sky. Yellow blossoms scattered across the reflection. The small boat sent ripples through the mirror and moored itself on the reflection's front door.

They got out wearily, stiff from long hours of rowing. They waded through reeds and water-lilies at the edge of the river, and Terje pulled the boat up onto the bank. As they gazed up uncertainly at the massive, open doors, a man stepped out of the house, came down the steps to greet them.

It was the Hunter.

He was dressed in a light green garment that fitted closely all over his body, like a second skin. But it was, Kyreol decided, no more peculiar than fur and face masks. She recognized him almost before she saw his face, by the way he moved, silently, gracefully, poised for sound. A smile broke over his face. He took Kyreol's hand gently—a peculiar gesture—and led her up the steps as though she had never climbed a tree in her life.

"Orcrow," she said in his own language. "I am happy to see you." She saw the surprise in his face and laughed. She explained carefully, "I learned from the stone. From Joran."

"Are you well?"

"Oh, yes. Very well."

"And you, Terje? You've grown."

"I know." He put his arm beside Kyreol's. "Look. I'm almost as dark as she is." Kyreol shook her head, laughing again, her fingers closing over his wrist for comfort as they crossed the threshold. The cool stillness of the place eased over them like water. They stopped.

"It's like the caves," Kyreol whispered after a moment. "Only—"

There were statues, slabs of painted stone resting on pedestals, woven baskets, masks peering down from the walls, weapons and shields behind transparent walls, many things from many dreams. Kyreol felt uneasy, suddenly. Her bare feet shifted on the stone floor.

"Only what?" Orcrow asked gently.

"There is no—the story is all broken up." She drew breath sharply, edging against Terje. Within one of the transparent cases on the far wall was a skirt of many-colored feathers. A betrothal skirt.

She put her hands over her mouth. How could such a thing from the Riverworld have travelled so far? "How—" Her voice caught. It was terrible to see, as though the Riverworld itself lay behind that case, dustless and unused, a small thing in an unfamiliar place. Terje put his arm around her shoulders.

"It's only a skirt." But his own voice shook.

"But how did it get here?"

"It was given to this house," Orcrow said softly.

"But nobody—no one in the Riverworld knew—"

"Kyreol, you aren't the first curious young woman to leave the Riverworld."

A thought touched her mind; she shook it away. "What kind of a place is this?"

"It's a dream-house," Terje said. His voice was certain again. "You see something in your mind, you make it real with your hands. After a while, it gets old, or broken, or you forget about it. Or else it makes its way here so other people can see the way you dreamed it." He gazed at Orcrow calmly, his hand patting Kyreol's shoulder, daring the Hunter to make the world more complicated.

But the faint worry in the Hunter's face eased. "Terje," he said in Terje's language, "you are wise as a Healer," and Terje blushed.

Someone else came to join them, then: a slender, red-haired man with a beard, wearing a body-skin like the Hunter's, only black. Kyreol stared at him. She had never seen red hair before, and only old men wore beards. His eyes were bright blue, smiling; his whole face looked warm, delighted to see her for some reason, making her smile back at him. He said something in a strange language to Orcrow, who said gravely to Kyreol,

"Kyreol, this is Arin Thrase. He collects all these things here and takes care of them. He can answer any questions you have about them." He paused, then added, "He studies the story behind each object: who made it, what it means."

Kyreol asked shyly, "What language does he speak?"

"The language of this part of the desert."

"Then where is your world? Still farther?" She felt tired suddenly, bewildered. "How far do I have to go?"

The Hunter was silent, as she had first seen him, all his thoughts hidden as he looked at her. The red-haired man murmured something, and the Hunter answered in his language. Arin Thrase left them quickly, his voice raised, calling for someone. Then, down a corridor, they heard him singing, his voice booming cheerfully, echoing off the stones.

"He said you looked hungry."

"Orcrow, where are we?" She pointed. "Is that my mother's betrothal skirt?"

"Yes."

There was a lump in Kyreol's throat. "Why did—why did she take it with her?"

"She was very young," the Hunter said gently. "Only a few years older than you. She left the River-world for many of the same reasons you did. Only she left alone. You left with Terje. She took a few things to remind her of where her home was. For comfort. Later, she gave this to Arin Thrase."

"She was here."

"No. She met him farther down the river."

Kyreol felt dizzy. She wanted to sit down, but there was no place to sit except on the stone floor. She glanced at Terje, who was standing very still, looking as though he were dreaming with his eyes open. He blinked, feeling her look, and put his arm around her shoulders.

"Then that's where you have to go," he said simply.

"Will you come with me?" Her eyes pleaded with him: If it's not too far? If you don't have to think about Moon-Flash?

"I won't leave you alone," he said. She felt the Hunter watching them then and gazed down at her fingers, then at him.

His face wore its remote, distant expression, as though he were listening to secrets. But he only said, "You need some clothes."

He went out among the diggers while Kyreol and Terje ate with Arin Thrase. The food was strange but good: a spicy stew with tender meat in it, sticky, sugary fruit, bread that was white instead of brown, and some kind of boiled green leaves. They sat in a room full of woven rugs and tapestries, and Kyreol kept glimpsing stories among the patterns of the colored threads. But she could ask no questions until the Hunter returned, so they ate quietly, shyly. When Orcrow came in finally, Kyreol said, "Oh," and pulled out the crystal. "I forgot." She opened it. Arin Thrase was staring at her amazedly. "Joran. It's Kyreol. We're here, in the big house."

"Good!" Joran said. "Have you met Arin Thrase?"

"Yes. He is feeding us. And the Hunter is here."

"Orcrow!" the stone exploded. "I want to talk—" The Hunter took the stone from Kyreol's hand.

"I'm here," he said. Arin Thrase was chuckling.

"Where have you been?"

"Where do you think I've been? I've been tracking two children down the longest river in the world. It's

101

the most miserable job I've ever had in my life, and I'm lucky I didn't get eaten alive, in case you're interested—"

"I'm not," the stone said grudgingly. "You should have taken them home."

"Why didn't you? You knew where they were. You could have picked them up any time, instead of letting me burn myself to a crisp under the sun. Why didn't you?"

"And do what?" Joran said exasperatedly. "Fly them home? To the Riverworld? In an air-shuttle?"

"All right," Orcrow said. "All right, then. Don't yell at me for coming to the same conclusion. It seemed better to let them go as far as they wanted."

"Well, now what are you going to do with them?"

"Ask Kyreol." He held the crystal out to catch her words.

"Kyreol," Joran said. "What do you want now? Do you want to go back home?"

"No," she said. "I want to see Orcrow's world."

"It's not that much farther," the Hunter said. The stone made a disgusted noise.

"Orcrow. It's light-years away. To them. She asked me what the Moon-Flash is. How are you going to tell her?"

Orcrow sighed. "She's the one who wants the answers. I'm sorry this happened, but she's the one who followed me. She saw beneath my disguise, she asked the questions. She left the Riverworld. There is a precedent."

The stone was silent. "All right," it said more quietly. "You handle it. And check in with Domecity headquarters—they've been at me every day, trying

102

to locate you. You're probably out of a job, but in view of your trek down the river to guard the children, they might let you scrape plates in a cafeteria somewhere."

"Thanks," the Hunter said drily. He added, "And they aren't children anymore." He closed the crystal, said something in Arin's language, and the red-haired man shook his head, smiling.

Orcrow gave Kyreol a long white skirt and a loose white shirt she could pull over her head. The cloth was tightly woven, very soft and light. It seemed to come from neither bird nor animal, and she wondered how it was made. There were too many things to wonder about. Terje put on the same kind of shirt, and a pair of pants that came only halfway to his knees, like the ones the men who were digging had been wearing. She remembered the tiny, isolated dust storms, then, and had the Hunter ask Arin,

"Why are they digging out there?"

"They're unburying a lost city," Arin said; and when she looked blank, he explained slowly, "Many years ago, a city was built out of stone beside the river. The people who lived then are all dead, and the desert winds buried the city beneath the earth. The people digging find many things: cups, bowls, jewelry, weapons, statues, painted walls, even bones from burial sites. Most of the things are broken, but we piece them together, carefully, so we can see what the people made. Come, I'll show you."

They followed him down one of the quiet, delicately painted hallways.

"Why are there dust clouds on the hills with no wind?"

The Hunter translated, and Arin laughed. "You don't miss much, do you, Kyreol?" He paused, then reached to a shelf and took down a small vase. "Suppose this were covered with dust. What would you do?"

Kyreol drew a breath and blew. The imaginary dust puffed into the air. She laughed, then looked surprised. "But I can't blow a cloud that big."

"No. But we make—things that blow for us out there. Very gently, so small things aren't disturbed. Wind covered them up, so we let the wind uncover them. It keeps the diggers from breaking things with their tools." He put the vase back and led them into a huge, sunlit room. It was, Kyreol thought, as if all the pots and knives and beads and bone bracelets, all the hunting traps and spears and carpets and children's toys in the Riverworld had all been gathered into one place, to be sorted out again. Long tables held piles of beads, bits of pottery, small broken statues, all waiting to be mended. A couple of people sat at the tables, piecing things together. They glanced up, smiling, then went back to their work.

"This is what we gather out of the diggings."

"But why?"

"To see how people before us lived. How they looked at this world. What they loved."

He took them through a doorway into another room. This one held things that at first glance meant very little; nothing about them said what they were for. There were sandstone pillars with odd signs on them, small painted stones, paintings on leather, shapeless carvings of wood and bone, masks without faces, fiery wheels of feathers. Kyreol, standing in the center of the room, felt as if she had suddenly gone deaf in a place full of chattering people. Arin watched her a moment, smiling. Then he took one of the stones off its shelf.

"What does that say to you?"

Kyreol held it in her hand. *Nothing.* The stone was as big as her palms, worn into a smooth oval, probably by the river. There was a black line down the center of it. "The story is in two parts," she said tentatively. She heard the Hunter translate to Arin. She added, remembering her dream, "Maybe it's a message to someone. On one side of the stone is a man. "No." She looked more closely. "It's a woman. There are little trees all around her. Maybe that's her sign. She lives among small trees. Then there is the black line. Then . . ." A blue line cut across the other side of the stone, with lean black smudges rising out of it and a tiny circle, like a black moon, rising over them. "I don't . . ." The breath went out of her suddenly "Oh . . . the faces. Beside the river. That's the message. Moon-Flash. This woman who lived among the little trees is dead. She's buried inside the faces."

She looked up at Arin, who took the stone from her gently. He was silent for a moment, then he said something to Orcrow, who nodded. Arin set the stone down.

"You have seen the faces."

"Yes."

"You touched them."

"Yes."

"Why?"

"Because—I wanted to know why people would make such huge stone faces. I just—I wanted to know."

Arin sighed audibly. She felt Terje's hand touch her, lightly. The Hunter said to her, "Arin has never seen the faces. He's seen pictures of them. For most people, the journey there is forbidden. He said that you have a great gift for understanding things people want to say without words. He thinks you should stay here. He can teach you many things."

"But—" Kyreol felt bewildered. Where was "here"? Here was only a pause in the river's movement, a place with no true name, a house that held only things that would never be used again, forgotten by the people who made them. The Hunter took her hands. His dark eyes looked deeply into hers.

"Kyreol. My world is very different. There, everything is spoken. Dreams mean nothing. If you see it, your eyes will change. You may never be able to look at the Riverworld again."

"You did," she whispered. Her throat burned. "You lived in both worlds. Why?"

9

THAT NIGHT, asleep beside Terje in the room full of tapestries, Kyreol dreamed she was flying on the back of a butterfly. She had seen a few tiny butterflies in the Riverworld, colored pale pink and green like the leaves of the River-Tree. This one was huge, with wings silky black as night; lights glowed in them like stars. It lifted her into the air, swooped with her; she clung to its antennae, laughing, unafraid even of its great, golden eyes. Then a voice like the voice from the crystal said, "Cleared," and, suddenly terrified, she groped behind her, saying, "Terje." He was there, unexpectedly; she felt his hand in hers. She woke up then and saw the tapestries settling lightly as wings in the morning breeze.

She lifted her head, saw Terje asleep. He was close to her, but she felt lonely, suddenly, as if the room were about to tear apart and float him away from her, still dreaming. Panicked, she said his name; he lifted his face out of the cushions, murmuring, blinking. He saw the fear in her face and reached for her hand. Then he shifted, pulling her against him, holding her closely, his arms around her, his cheek against her cheek. But it wasn't enough. She still felt far from him, as though time and water and the earth itself were between them; she couldn't get close enough to feel safe.

"My bones are afraid," she whispered.

"Did you have a dream?"

"I don't know why." Then she laughed a little at herself, because she couldn't imagine where so much fear might come from. The laughter made her feel better. "Terje," she said, thinking of what might lie ahead of them, "I was never afraid until now."

"Yes, you were."

"Not like this. Not of things I haven't even seen."

"Your mother has seen them," he said, and the thought comforted her a little.

"Yes. I wonder . . . I wonder if she'll like me."

Terje stared at her. The expression on his face was so comical she laughed again, and the fear finally dwindled away. Then there was a silence between them as they looked at one another. The breeze seemed to still; the sunlight seemed the world might never be the same. Their faces drifted toward each other, like small boats in slowly moving water. Before they touched, the silence broke. They heard footsteps, Arin Thrase singing.

Terje's breath drained softly out of him. His mouth crooked. He drew Kyreol against his chest; she listened to his heartbeat, felt him kiss her hair. She closed her eyes, feeling close to him at last, safe for a while.

"Terje."

He made a noise.

"When we see the Hunter's world, then we'll know what to do. When we come to the end of the river."

Arin opened their door then, bringing them breakfast.

When they left his treasure house to go downriver, they saw that their boat was no longer moored among the waterlilies. Arin gestured toward a small dock bobbing along the river's edge.

"It will be safe there," Orcrow said. "We'll take a faster boat." He was no longer the Hunter, Kyreol sensed. His face belonged to his own world; already his eyes were seeing it. Arin Thrase took her hand, put something into it.

It was a tiny painted stone, shaped like a raindrop, a hole bored at one end so she could wear it around her neck. A yellow dot rising over a line of blue . . . It made her smile.

"Good fortune," Arin said, in the language of the Riverworld. He added something that Orcrow translated.

"If you want to come back here, you will always be welcome." He dropped his arms around their shoulders. "Come. This is the shortest and the longest journey."

They stepped into a boat, which wasn't made of wood. It was bright red, and like the crystal, it could talk. Kyreol sat down with a thump on one of the cushions in it. Orcrow offended the boat; it roared beneath them angrily and went backwards instead of forwards. Kyreol shrieked and tried to hide in the carpet on the floor of the boat. Terje slid down beside her, but Orcrow, implacable, eased the boat smoothly away from the dock. He turned a wheel in his hands, and the boat turned, picked up speed, and skimmed down the river, still thundering beneath them, tearing swatches of water into the air.

After a while, Kyreol realized that Terje was no longer huddled beside her. She lifted her head unhappily, feeling surrounded by the giant heartbeat of the boat. Terje was standing up beside Orcrow, watching the water part before them. Kyreol stared at him, amazed and annoyed. He was grinning. He had completely forgotten her. She got to her feet slowly. The wind and water whipped at her, but she moved forward, under the canopy, clear as air, hard as wood, that shielded them from the wind.

Orcrow moved a red stick, and the boat slowed, its voice softening. He glanced back, his face distant, almost hard. When he found Kyreol on her feet, he stopped the boat, let it drift in the water.

They heard river noises again, birds, the rustle of trees. Orcrow went to Kyreol, took her shoulders.

"Many things will frighten you now," he said. "But this is what you wanted. I'm giving you what you asked for. Just remember: you are safer with me than you have ever been since you reached Fourteen Falls. And before I let anything harm you, I would die first."

Kyreol swallowed. Her chin lifted; she lied with dignity, though he could see her still shaking. "Nothing in your world can make me afraid, Orcrow." Then, as he smiled, she asked perplexedly, "But how does it work?"

He set the boat purring beneath them, moving sedately, and tried to explain. To explain, he had to teach them new words. Kyreol learned them patiently, though she could have thought up a far better story of how the boat with the bellowing voice moved so quickly through the water.

Then Terje wanted to drive the boat. When Kyreol protested, he said, "It's simple. When you turn the wheel, the boat turns. When you push the red stick up, it goes faster. When you push it down, it slows."

"Is that all?" She turned to Orcrow. "Why didn't you just say that?"

He sighed.

They spent that night on the riverbank under the stars, as they had done so many nights before. They built a fire and heated food that Arin had given them. Kyreol found it hard to sleep. The boat had unlocked all the noise in the world. The river chattered in a strange language; night birds made harsh noises. Even the sky spoke occasionally, droning like a mosquito. She got up finally, restlessly, and walked away from the river, homesick for the first time for the small peaceful noises of the Riverworld, for trails she could walk at night with her eyes closed, that led from one safe spot to another. She went through a grove of trees, so quietly she didn't wake the birds, and up a small hill until she could barely hear the noise of the river.

She stood in the moonlight, searching the face of the moon, and it comforted her. It was tranquil and serene, the message-stone of the night, painted crystal-white, meaning peace. She wondered, for the first time, if it wouldn't have been wiser not to ask so many questions if the answers were so confusing, so full of change and noise. Maybe she should go back . . . Her eyes strayed away from the moon, followed stars down to the edge of the horizon. But they didn't stop there. Thousands upon thousands of stars glittered on the dark earth, in the distance, on both sides of the river.

She sat down slowly on the cool, hard ground. Something enormous hovered above the lights. Big as a mountaintop, shaped like a half-moon tipped over ... like a dome. Its underside was ringed with lights. It was dark, shadowy, smoldering from within with white fire, blue fire. Tiny burning insects winged in and out of it ...

She huddled against herself, hugged her knees tightly, pushed her face against them. There were no stories for such a thing. There was only truth. The Hunter had told her that. The Riverworld was so small it could have been lost among those stars and never found. Once it had been the entire world. Now it was no bigger compared to the world than her thumbnail was to her.

"You wanted to know," she whispered to herself. "You wanted to know." She lifted her head again, crying helplessly, out of fear, for lost tales, until, in her blurring tears, the vast thing in the sky took on a fiery beauty such as she had never seen. She wiped her eyes, gazing at it, glimpsing the strangeness of the Hunter's world. It meant nothing. It was itself. It held no messages, it had no need of stories. It was an answer.

She stirred finally and found the Hunter, sitting quietly as a stone, not far from her. She blinked at him, wondering how—wondering why ...

"Why did you learn to move like that?" she whispered.

"To become a hunter."

"In your world?"

"In yours."

"Why?"

He shifted to sit beside her, said softly, "Kyreol, the Riverworld is tiny, but its names and rituals are far older than that city. Many people know it exists. Very, very few are ever permitted to go there. I was one permitted. We go . . . because the Riverworld, its tales, its way of life, is something we value. Something precious. We go occasionally, secretly, disturbing no one, to make certain that nothing we do under that great dome disturbs the Riverworld. Not only the Riverworld, but all the small worlds within the world. We go even among the mask-people, among the river-tribe who built the faces. It's a harsh, difficult thing to do. Sometimes it's dangerous. But we go not to bring knowledge, not to bring change, but to observe. To watch over these little worlds. To guard their peace." His face eased a little. "That's why when you and Terje left the Riverworld because of me, the people in that dome were so angry with me. I should never have disturbed you, never caused you to question. But, having caused that, now I'm responsible for you."

My mother—is she there?"

"She came there, yes. Only . . . she came alone down that river. She never saw the stranger in the River-world. As you did. She simply asked, 'Where does the river go?' And she got into a boat and followed it."

Kyreol smiled a little, wiping at dried tears. "I'm more afraid than she was."

"Kyreol, you and Terje have so much courage you fill me with wonder."

"Terje . . ." She plucked a grass stem at her feet, tore it delicately along its seam. "He—we—"

"I know. You love him. And you are betrothed." He chuckled as she stared at him. "I'm trained to know about the Riverworld."

"He is to be betrothed, at the next Moon-Flash."

The Hunter was silent for a long time. "What does he want to do?"

"I don't know. He doesn't know. He—" She frowned at the grass pieces, twisting them together. "He doesn't want to trouble the Riverworld either. To disturb its rituals. Sometimes I think he never left it. All this is the dream. The betrothal at Moon-Flash—that's the way things really are. Not this." The immense floating dome drew her eyes again. Lights pulsated; it swallowed tiny flying things like a fish. "What is it for?"

"It's for—it's like the dock where the boats were moored. Only—"

She turned to him, her eyes big. "The things that fly like birds—they're boats? Boats for the air?"

"Ships."

"Ships."

"Yes. Some of them come from other worlds. Other earths." He gestured across the endless span of stars. "From there. They make their journeys down the river of the stars to come to Domecity."

"It's a story," she breathed, entranced. "You're telling me a story."

"Some of the animals you saw along the river were from other worlds. Worlds too crowded, too busy to take care of them. So they were sent here, to live freely in the wilderness." He touched her hair lightly, smiling at the look on her face. "Do you like the story?"

She nodded. "Oh, yes. What does my mother do here?"

"She—" The Hunter's voice stopped the story. "I think she should tell you. It's not easy for me to explain." He stood up, then; she watched him. He held out his hand, a dark, still figure in the night, as she had first seen him.

"Hunter," she whispered.

"Yes."

She let him pull her to her feet, stood beside him, gazing down at the city of stars.

The next day, they began to see people along the riverbanks. The river grew wide; houses of bewildering shape and size crusted its banks. There were no silent places anymore. The hot air seemed to throb with a dull, constant boom, like a heartbeat growing louder and louder. Boats crowded into the water, eluding each other in a graceful, unspoken ritual. Some were beautiful, catching the breeze with colored wings. Some sped and roared; others dropped out of the air like dragonflies, drew in their feet, unfurled their wings, and loosed fishing lines as they moved upriver. Terje, trying to drive and stare at the same time, almost hit one of them. A man on it yelled unknown words at him. Orcrow took the wheel, and Terje sank down beside Kyreol on the cushions. His body looked tense, defensive, as though all the sounds and colors were storming at him. Kyreol, watching him, wondered if his face would ever become quiet again. Then, slowly, he changed, something inside of him flowing outward, a current of peace, protecting him from the world.

"How do you do that?" she asked. He looked at her out of calm eyes.

"Do what?"

"Whatever it is you're doing."

"I'm not doing anything."

"Well, what were you thinking about?"

He scratched his head. "I don't know. All the different shapes the world makes."

They saw buildings steep and high as cliffs and others the same shape as the little turtle-shell houses of the Riverworld, only a hundred times bigger. Some buildings twisted themselves into peculiar shapes; their colors were smooth, bright, glistening like water. Factories, Orcrow called them. They made everything, he explained. Boats, the cloth they were wearing, airships. The air above them hummed busily, looking as crowded as the water. Finally, rounding a curl in the river, Kyreol saw the dome again.

It looked translucent by day, floating like a cloud, catching sunlight on its rim. It was barely visible, a fragile half-bubble, so light it might be pushed with one hand. Ships buzzed in and out of it like bees. Now and then a tiny violet patch appeared in the bubble and swallowed a ship. Airy as it seemed, its walls blocked out the sky.

"Reflectors underneath it catch the sunlight," Orcrow said mysteriously, "and pour it down over the city." He showed her, angling sunlight into his palm with a piece of metal. "Otherwise it would cast too great a shadow." Kyreol, dizzied by the constant, incomprehensible variety of the city, too numb to ask questions, nodded wordlessly. Orcrow glanced at her sharply. "We're almost there."

"Where?" she asked helplessly. "Orcrow, I've never seen so many words I don't know."

"I know." He withdrew the crystal from a pocket and spoke into it. They were going slowly now, because the river was so crowded, and faces, skin-colorings, clothes on other boats were clearly visible. Sometimes Kyreol heard words she understood, carried at random across the water.

"Channel two. Regny Orcrow. Open channel to airdock six, please, channel to airdock six."

"Regny Orcrow," the stone said in a woman's voice. "Acknowledged. All channels closed to that name except channel one priority, one priority. Please contact the Dome."

Orcrow closed the stone. He stood silently a moment, his face the Hunter's face again: unreadable, contemplating distant movements. Then he flicked the stone open again. "Regny Orcrow. Channel one priority."

The stone spoke in a woman's voice again, but this was soft, husky, with a way of pronouncing words carefully, as if they were always new. "Channel one. Orcrow." Unlike Joran, she didn't shout at him; her voice was very grave. "Are the children safe?"

"They're with me. They're quite safe."

"Where are you?"

"Still on the river. We've entered Domecity. They're tired and hungry."

"No doubt."

"I think I should tell you—"

The stone broke into his words. "An air-shuttle will be waiting for you at airdock six. Please maintain contact with the Dome. I must warn you that at any moment I cannot contact you, you may be liable to prosecution. You will proceed to the Dome for a full inquiry into your astonishing lack of judgment. The children, of course, will not be submitted to airflight. I'll send someone from the Cultural Agency who speaks their language to meet them at the airdock."

"I'd rather not leave them."

"It seems to me," the voice said severely, "that they have already seen far too much of you."

Orcrow sighed. "I can't imagine what I did in the Riverworld to get myself recognized. But having inadvertently caused them to leave, please remember that I did everything in my power to keep them from harm. Please believe me when I tell you that under the circumstances, there was nothing I could do but permit the children to come to Domecity."

"Under what circumstances?"

"Kyreol. She's here beside me." He waited; the stone was silent. A breeze wrinkled across the water. In the silence, they passed from sunlight into the shadow of the Dome. "Nara," said Orcrow gently, and Kyreol's hands turned cold. Terje lifted his head slowly, blinking.

"Bring them to the Dome," the woman said.

10

THEY FLEW, as Kyreol had flown in her dream. Only it wasn't a butterfly, but a craft of silver, which winked and glowed within and spoke to itself. Kyreol, strapped to a seat, huddled against herself, pushed her hands against her eyes as she felt the earth fall away from her. She heard Orcrow talking in her own language; she felt Terje's arm on her shoulders. But the Hunter's words made no more sense than birds fluttering around her head, and fear lay like a chasm between her and Terje's arm. *I've left the River*, she kept thinking. *I've left the River. How will I ever get back?* Then another shock of cold would go through her. *The woman's name is Nara. Nara of the Dome. Or is it Nara of the River-Tree?* She lifted her head finally, jerkily, and interrupted Orcrow's noises.

"Is that my mother?"

"Yes," Orcrow said, and went on talking, but "yes" was all she heard. *Nara.* She saw her own dark face in her mind, heard the low, careful voice again. Then the voice out of her dream said, "Cleared." Blinking, she saw the Dome yawn open in front of them, and she hid her eyes again.

"Kyreol," Terje said. "Kyreol." She heard him dimly, as though she were dreaming. "Kyreol." She realized suddenly that the ship had stopped. People were standing; a hatch had opened. "Kyreol."

She drew a deep breath. Orcrow was gazing at her anxiously. He unfastened the strap across her quickly. Her whole body was tense; her fingers clung like bird claws to the arms of the seat. She heard herself say shakily, "I was afraid, Orcrow."

"It's all right."

She looked up at Terje wistfully. "Weren't you afraid?"

His face was so white it might have shown in the dark like a moon. "You didn't give me a chance." He coaxed her up. She closed her eyes again, envisioning the airy nothingness the Dome rested upon.

"Kyreol," Orcrow said. "The world itself floats like a bubble in space."

"I didn't know," she whispered. Her lips felt numb. She took a step and didn't fall through clouds. She took another. "Orcrow . . . How—how can people build things like this?"

She saw them both smile, as in relief. Then she saw her mother.

It was as though she looked into water and saw her own reflection. Only her reflection was dressed like Orcrow, like the people of Domecity. Her hair was drawn severely back from her face and knotted on top of her head. She belonged to a world of airships and dwellings that floated above the air. But her skin was black as the gleaming, water-carved walls of the Face,

120

and her eyes, as she gazed at Kyreol, were overflowing with memories.

Her voice was the gentle, careful voice of the stone. "My little Kyreol." Then she brushed at her tears and slowly, tentatively, Kyreol smiled.

Nara led them out of the silver ship, through a door at the dockwall, into a tiny room whose doors closed like a mouth. Nara spoke to the room; it rose upward, unsettling Kyreol's stomach. Ships that flew, rooms that moved and understood words . . . How did people dream such things? The doors opened again; they entered a vast domed room full of light.

"This is the very top of the Dome," Nara said. "This is where I live."

Trees and flowers dwelled under the soft light of the tinted roof. Fountains and small pools sparkled among the leaves. The trees didn't seem to mind being detached from the earth; they gathered light eagerly into their many-colored leaves. But they had forgotten how to speak; there was no wind. Doors circled the walls. People came in and out of them, their voices muted among the growing things. Some of them, catching sight of Nara and Kyreol together, stared in amazement. Kyreol could see the wonder, the questions in thir faces. *The children—the Riverworld children. How dared they leave the River to float higher than a mountain above the earth? What will they do now? What language do they speak? Can they live without wind?* But they only smiled a welcome and left Nara to ask their questions.

Nara opened a door in the circle of doors. Kyreol, stepping inside, had an impression of light, bird cries, green growing things. The room seemed full of leaves, like a forest. She blinked. Then she realized the bright birds were caged; the trees and ferns were in pots. Nara, watching her, smiled a little, almost shyly.

"I made a tiny Riverworld for myself," she explained. "Except there is no water." On the wall beside the bird cage hung familiar things: a painted leather amulet, a necklace of seeds, feather ankle-bracelets, a gold feather vest. Nara followed Kyreol's gaze. "I was married in that vest. I lost the marriage skirt, coming downriver, when my boat overturned."

"What did you do then?" Terje asked. Memories came into her eyes again.

"I made a raft. I had a bundle of clothes—I found them farther down, snagged on the bank."

"Your betrothal skirt," Kyreol said abruptly. Nara nodded surprisedly. Kyreol thought of her, homeless and alone on the great river, not knowing where it might take her. "You didn't have a speaking stone."

"No. Not then. Nor a Hunter. Sit down." They sat on the soft carpet among the trees. But she didn't move; she was looking at them as though she were trying to understand how they could have changed so from the children she had held. "Terje, do you remember me at all?"

He nodded, frowning a little. "I think so," he said shyly. "You used to—you used to tell us stories. Like Kyreol does now. You took us with you when you went to find herbs for—for the Healer." His face had flushed scarlet. "You—then you weren't there anymore. Ever. We looked for you . . . We thought you must be somewhere. Behind the next tree. The next rock. We would meet you at the next bend in the River. I would go to your house and think, *This morn-*

ing Kyreol's mother will open the door for me. But—"
He shrugged a little. "You never did." He added huskily, remembering, "We were so small."

Nara's head bowed. "I missed you," she said to
Kyreol, in the language of the Riverworld. "Going
down the River, I cried for you."

Kyreol's eyes filled. "How could you do it? At least
I had Terje with me."

"Aren't you angry with me for leaving you?"

"No. I was sad for a long time. That went away
and, after another long time, when my—when my
father said you weren't dead, I started to wonder
where you went. Where the River went."

"You . . . How did he know?" Nara said wonderingly.

"He had a dream."

"Of me? Here?"

"He dreamed a beautiful stone opened and said
your name. And you followed it into the sky. He never
said your name during the chants for the dead." She
added, "When I saw Orcrow for the first time, he was
talking to a stone. So I thought of my father's dream.
I started to wonder if it were the same stone. If the
Hunter knew you."

Orcrow made a soft sound in the back of his throat.
"They live in our past," he murmured. "Yet they
dream of us."

Nara was smiling again. "So you asked the Hunter
with the stone. When I left, you had just begun to
talk, and already you were asking questions. All day
long, you would bring me things. A leaf, a berry, a
frog. 'What is this? What is that?' You weren't happy
until I answered, until I gave you a word to learn.
And you made me remember all the questions I had

123

inside me when I was growing up. I wanted to find someone who could answer my simple questions the way I could answer yours." She shook her head a little. "I thought I could go a little way and come back. I didn't know that once you leave the Riverworld, you can never return."

There was a silence. Kyreol swallowed. "It's easy. I mean, it won't be easy because of the people and animals, but you just follow the water—"

"Well." Nara looked as though she was sorry for what she had said. "We can talk about that later—"

"But Terje—he has to be home at the next Moon-Flash. He has to be betrothed to Jage."

"Moon-Flash." Nara's eyes went past her then, to Orcrow. There was almost an appeal in them. Orcrow drew breath audibly, in response to some question hidden in the air. Terje shifted. His face seemed calm, and the edge of fear in Kyreol died away. He doesn't believe her, she thought. Why should he? The River is the River, and it will lead him home. She felt confused again, suddenly lonely, as if he had already left her, and then he met her eyes. He looked annoyed. She felt her cheeks burn.

"Jage," Nara murmured. "Jage. Oh, I remember. Of the Turtle-Crossing family."

Kyreol nodded, a different well of emotion making her forget the problem of returning. "That's what I've been wanting to ask you. Why did you betroth me to Korre instead of to Terje?"

"But Kyreol," Nara said, half-laughing. "I did that the day after you were born. How could I have known you and Terje would become so close?"

"That made me angry," Kyreol said darkly.

"I'm sorry."

"That's all right."

"It's hard," Nara said apologetically, "when babies are so tiny, to know who they might grow up to love."

"I suppose so."

"And most Riverworld children are very much alike."

"Except us."

There was a little silence. Nara was smiling, but there was a faint worried expression in her eyes, as though she were seeing something even more confusing than everything the River had led toward. It made Kyreol uneasy again. She moved, then touched Terje impulsively, drawing from his calm.

For some reason, that made the worry in Nara's eyes deepen. But she only said, "You must be very hungry. I'll get some food."

She went into the next room. After a moment, she called, "Regny, there are all kinds of messages for you on my channel. Call the North Outstation, call Arin Thrase, call the Cultural Agency, call Domecity security, call the Dome Comcenter to clear your calls. And call home."

Orcrow sighed. "I almost wish I were back in the desert." He joined Nara, leaving Kyreol and Terje among the silent trees.

Terje spoke finally, breaking their own amazed silence. "I just wanted to see the rainbows . . ."

"Terje."

"What?"

"What did she mean we can't go home? I was afraid to ask."

Terje stared at her so incredulously she smiled. But

her brows were still puckered. He shrugged. "I don't know. I don't think she meant—"

"Because you have to go home."

"Will you stop saying that!" The sudden anger in his voice startled her. They faced each other silently again, tensely. Then he picked at the green carpet and the flush faded out of his face. "Do you think I want to leave you?"

"But Terje," she said in a small voice.

"I followed you all the way down the River. I'm sitting here with you beyond the edge of the world—"

"Pretend it's a dream," she said helplessly. "You'll wake up, and there will be Jage—"

His voice rose again. "Why?"

"Because what will you do here? There's no place to fish. The birds are caged. The River ended. You only came to see rainbows—"

"Kyreol." He stopped and sighed. "You aren't making any sense. What are you thinking? That nobody will notice that I vanished with you one day and came back without you? You think they won't ask why?"

"I don't want them to ask!" she said vehemently. "Anything!"

"Then what do you—"

"I don't want any changes! You go back, you marry Jage, and never say anything—never tell anyone. Oh, Terje—" she cried softly, as his face began to understand. "I want the Riverworld to be always alive. I never want it locked behind cases or nailed to walls. You go back, you keep it alive."

"I can't," he said softly, reaching out to her. She

126

shifted, pushed herself close to him, her eyes wide, unseeing.

"I'm afraid again," she whispered.

"Of what?"

"I don't know. Terje, the Riverworld itself is like something kept in Arin Thrase's house. It's guarded, protected, just like my mother's betrothal skirt—"

"No."

"Yes. We—we look at the world one way. A simple way for a tiny world. But I wonder what—how these people look at the world. They watch our world so it doesn't change. But what is it they see surrounding the Riverworld? They see something. That's why they won't let us go back. Because they know something— something that can't live in the Riverworld. And if we stay here long enough, we'll—"

"Kyreol, how can you say that?" he protested softly. "How can that be true?"

"Why else did my mother say we couldn't go back?"

"Do you want to go back?"

"I want—" She stopped, frowning at the deepening shades of green in the carpet. Then her face cleared a little and she sighed, leaning back against Terje's shoulder. "I don't want to give anything up. I wish I could be here and there at the same time. And you What do you want?"

He scratched his head. "I would like a boat like Orcrow's," he said, and she shifted, laughing.

"Terje—"

"I do. And I want—" His hands moved vaguely in the air. "It's hard to say. I want . . . just to live. To see new worlds, or see the same world, and know that everything is new. Or that there's no difference. Between this world and the Riverworld. Everything is the same. The dreams change shape, but the dreamer never changes."

She was silent, her lips parted, glimpsing now and then what he was trying to say. She turned her face, kissed him, as though she could understand him that way. "But Terje," she said tentatively, feeling stupid, "what do you want to do?"

He smiled. But he looked a little bewildered, too. Nara came in then, with trays of steaming dishes. The smells were familiar: fish stew, warm bread made with nut flour, a sauce of berries and plums. There were even wild honeycombs to dip the bread into. Kyreol, aching with hunger, remembered the sound of bees swarming on a sun-soaked afternoon, with the green River dreaming in the distance. She saw herself picking up Korre's little sisters, telling them stories . . . Where was that Kyreol now? *Maybe I should have stayed*, she thought. There was no reason not to love something so simple.

"Eat," Nara said gently. Kyreol broke off a piece of bread, got it past the burning in her throat, and felt better.

Orcrow joined them again, looking tired. "I told the Agency I was back. They seemed surprised that you were feeding me instead of firing me. I tried to explain to them that the lure of the world drew the children, not some stranger wandering around their home dressed in feathers. But all they can envision is two terrified children, like aliens off another planet, understanding nothing."

"I don't understand anything," Kyreol said with

dignity. "But I'm not terrified. Will they stop you from going back to the Riverworld?"

"They want to," Orcrow said. "But the final decision is your mother's. She is the head of the branch of the Agency that watches over the people along the river. And she trained me." He filled his plate, but didn't eat. With his head bowed, his hands motionless, he seemed to be waiting for Nara's judgment.

"Orcrow," she said softly, "you brought my child safely down the river to me. When I was young, going down that river, not even the thought of the baby I left behind could stop me. I was very angry with you at first. I trained you; I couldn't understand how you could have let such a thing happen. But since it was my own child you brought me, I know that if you hadn't been there, she would have gone alone. And perhaps not survived. So all I can do is thank you. Besides," she added, as his face eased into a smile, "I want you to go back to the Riverworld."

The smile vanished. "Now? I just got here."

"I know. But this time you can fly home. I want you to—"

"Icrane," he said abruptly, and she nodded, looking away from him.

"I want—first I disappeared. And then his daughter. I want—"

"What do you want?" he asked gently. "Do you want me to tell him where you are?"

There was a little silence. "It's against the law," she said reluctantly, but she still couldn't meet his eyes. "Orcrow, I was his wife. The wife of the Healer of the Riverworld. He knows I'm alive. He can't even mourn me and then forget me. And now Kyreol has left him, too. And Terje. You know the Riverworld. I won't ask you to break the law, but just—somehow— let him know that we're safe and well."

Kyreol said suddenly, "You sent him a message, Orcrow. I dreamed it."

He gazed at her silently. "I left him a stone."

"With three signs painted on it. So he would know I was alive and making my mother's journey." She added, "You could give him another message like that. You know that language."

He drew breath, turning again to Nara. "You see? They dream our thoughts, they reach out to our world. If children of people who know nothing at all about the world are driven within themselves to explore it, I wonder how long we will be able to disguise ourselves among them. It seems wrong to me that the law should forbid a man's wife to travel across the world to see him once again. I'll return, of course. I'll find some way to tell him. But I think we should begin to go openly at least to the Riverworld, tell them the truth about ourselves. Perhaps then they can teach us to dream again."

"Perhaps," Nara said softly, and gave them a glimpse, for a brief moment, of the longing she still felt for her home. "But, Regny, the very peace and orderliness of their lives might be the source of their dream-power. If we disturb that, we might destroy the very thing we are searching for. Besides, how could we begin to tell them the truth? Where does truth begin, in the Riverworld? With a dream? A place-name? A fire on the moon?"

"You wouldn't have to tell them that—"

"That the Moon-Flash they worship, which blesses

their betrothals, brings good fortune, good hunting, children, is no more than . . ." Her voice faltered suddenly. Kyreol, her hands frozen above her food, felt her mother's attention even before Nara turned her head slowly, reluctantly, to meet Kyreol's eyes. Kyreol wanted to speak, but her lips refused to shape the words. *What? No more than what?* As though Nara's words held her under a spell, she couldn't even blink. Nara continued finally, shaping her words very carefully, her voice thread-thin, as though it hurt her to speak, ". . . the flare of a supply ship's engines as it makes its final descent to the moon. As it has done every year, on the same night, for four hundred and seventy-nine years, since the Dome realized that people of this world had begun to worship it."

11

AS IN A DREAM, Kyreol felt herself surrounded by night-shadowed people of the Riverworld, their faces turned toward the full moon rising above the white, feathery water rolling down the Face. Fire struck the moon's side, and small drums began to sound. She saw the Sun-Woman's blue cheek with the Moon-Flash painted on it, the sign on the desert boy's painted wrist, the circle and the flame carved into black rock that cradled within it a dead man's bones. Moon-Flash. Life, betrothal, ritual, love, power, death.

"A ship." Her voice made no sound. "Like the one that brought us up here."

"Yes."

"It makes a fire——"

"Before it lands. To slow it down, so it won't crash."

"That's all? Just a ship landing?" She shook her head a little, jerkily. Her cheeks felt hot. "But we——I was betrothed at Moon-Flash. The moon moves to its position among the stars, and we begin to chant——"

"I know," Nara said huskily. "I have chanted to the moon."

"And then a ship lands on the moon, and we think it's our good fortune; but it's not, it's just somebody else's ship—"

"Maybe it is your good fortune. Because you believe it's true, you make it true. Oh, Kyreol." She reached out, took Kyreol's hands between her own, her eyes pleading for understanding, or perhaps forgiveness. "There were people in a city on the moon needing supplies. So long ago, they needed many things. So ships were sent. And gradually, people like Orcrow who studied other cultures began finding the Moon-Flash symbol in carvings, paintings, in rituals. When they finally realized what it was, they began sending the big supply ship on the same night every year. Now, sometimes the ships aren't even needed; they might carry very little, or nothing. But they're still sent. Because if the moon people don't need them, the River-people do."

Kyreol stared down at the carpet. "We thought the moon blessed us. And that the world began at the Face and ended at Fourteen Falls, and rainbows grew like flowers you could pick . . ." A bird cried in its cage behind her. She was on her feet suddenly; she saw Terje's head jerk up, his shaggy hair swinging free of his face, but she moved before she saw the expression in it. Orcrow stood, upsetting the tray, but she was too quick for him. The door opened as she came toward it. She heard her mother call her name. And then, in a sudden flurry of bird cries, she was free.

Kyreol, she thought, *of the Riverworld*, and all she remembered of hidden trailings, secret flights, games of stealth and silence in the forests came back to her. She disappeared like a shadow into the trees. But

Terje knew her too well, and Orcrow was a trained Hunter, so she had to make choices fast. She heard laughter and ducked behind a plant pot. Then she saw doors in the far wall open. People walked out of one of the tiny, shifting rooms. The doors snapped shut again. She moved toward them.

When they opened, emptying themselves of people, she ran forward, out of the trees. In the brief moments before the doors closed behind her, she turned and saw Orcrow staring at her from across the room. His hand went out to her. She saw his mouth move. *Wait, Kyreol!* She jumped back, panicked, and remembered to speak to the room. It couldn't go up any farther, so she said, "Down." The doors closed as Orcrow began to run.

In the silence, Kyreol leaned against the wall and listened to her heartbeat. The room made its private journey through the Dome; she didn't know where it would stop. She wished she could stay in it for a while, like a turtle in its shell. She wanted to sit beside the River again, throw stones in it until the world sorted itself out again and she found her place in it once more.

But the room stopped abruptly. The doors opened; two women walked in, talking. They fell silent as they saw Kyreol, startled by something in her face. But she edged past them quickly, seeing shadows, quiet spaces beyond the doors. The room went on its way. She stood without breathing, staring upward.

A waterfall made of light poured down from the ceiling. It made no noise, it began and ended nowhere. It fell endlessly, blazing rose, gold, the icy-blue of stars. But there was no water, no stones, no rainbows.

Her throat began to ache again and unshed tears. *What is this place?* she thought. *The trees don't talk, the water isn't wet. Nothing is real. Not even the Moon-Flash. The River is real, but I can't get to it. Or maybe it isn't real. Maybe it doesn't even know our names; maybe it doesn't even know the fish . . . I wish Terje was here. I'm alone, without even the stone, in a place where all the words are new.*

She saw a passageway beyond the lightfall and crept toward it soundlessly. As she entered it, she began to hear voices. She hid herself and peered around a corner.

Light struck her eyes almost blindingly. Her stomach lurched. She was looking out into space through a window in the Dome wall. A cloud had hurt her eyes. The Dome seemed to rest on it, a whorled, airy field softer than bird down, softer than a child's breath . . . She could have curled deep into it and slept if the sun, hidden behind a shield in the wall, hadn't set the cloud on fire. She heard voices again and dragged her eyes away from the brilliance.

The big room was full of paintings. But the paintings moved, glowed, changed, spoke. Half-a-dozen people moved among them, speaking to each other, occasionally to the images of ships, clouds, lights, random patterns that flicked endlessly within their frames. One man, eating something as he spoke, touched a cluster of lights in front of a moving ship.

"YL1415 cleared for entry, gate two. 978TS, your fuel lane is cleared. Take it slow . . . What's that? Who?" The image changed to a streak of light. "Computer, we need a translator channel open to 5.97." He called over his shoulder, "Someone coming in from Xtal."

Kyreol edged back through the passageway and went to sit behind the lightfall. The world was impossible. She could hardly tell if the men in there spoke the same language she had learned from the stone. And how could they ever care about a single Moon-Flash? They had a thousand magic lights and were unawed by all of them. How they must laugh at the Riverworld for honoring a ship's fire. She put her face against her knees. *How could they let us believe that, for so many years? It was only a story. The whole Riverworld is nothing but a story.* She heard her mother's words: "Because you believe it's true, you make it true." But was even that true? A ship's landing-fire was a ship's landing-fire, no matter how much you chanted to it. She stirred restlessly after a while and slipped out of her hiding place.

She found another of the small moving rooms and told it to take her down. She didn't know where she was going. *Back to the River? I can't live under this moon*, she thought. *But* . . . The thought pursued her like a shadow. *There is no other moon. I can't stay here. I can't go home. I don't know what to do.*

"Kyreol," the room said suddenly. "Kyreol." Kyreol jumped, clung to the wall. Above her head, an amber light was flashing. "Kyreol, please return to the top of the Dome."

Kyreol put her hands over her eyes. The room stopped speaking, stopped moving. Its doors opened. Kyreol dodged past the people entering without looking at them. A voice snatched at her, but she ran on

136

until she heard nothing but the sound of her feet on carpets.

She looked up. She was surrounded by closed doors. They were all alike, all shiny black in the pale walls, with the same seam down the center of them. They were like closed mouths, giving her no answers. She imagined going through one and finding her father behind it, kneeling on his carpet of River-signs, pouring her tea for her.

Sit down, Kyreol, he might say. *Dream for me.*

Dream? But there was nothing left to dream. She ran again, past all the closed doors, down the curved, silent corridor until it widened abruptly in front of her.

Smells, voices rolled over her. More people than she had ever seen together in her life were crowded in one room. They were getting food out of the walls and eating it. All the smells jumbled together, making her feel sick. *What can they be eating?* she wondered. *Was it ever alive? Or can they tell?* She remembered picking berries in the morning light along the river-banks. Then she saw someone look at her and rise, still watching her. She turned quickly.

There was another corridor angling away from the feeding-room. She ran down that, searching for more moving-rooms. *I can go down,* she thought, *keep going down until I can't go any farther in the tiny rooms. That's where the ships are. I'll hide in one and let it take me back to the River. When I see the River again, I'll be able to think what to do. There's no place to think up here. I wish Terje were here.*

She saw another travelling room finally. But someone stood directly in front of it. She ducked back behind a corner and peered out. The man stood with his back to the doors. Something in the expression on his face reminded Kyreol of a hunter stilling himself for a long wait. *He's watching for something*, she thought, and then knew what it was. *Me.*

She turned, ducked down another hallway and found another guard. She leaned against the wall in the shadows, panting. *Why won't they let me go? I just want to get back to the River.* She thought of Terje and of Orcrow and her mother, whom she was leaving behind, but they all seemed far away, people from a dream. *I'll come back to them. But first I have to get to the River.*

She found a moving room finally that wasn't guarded. She told it to go down and it went down, but not far enough. Its doors opened; she looked out. There were no ships, only a corridor like many others. She spoke to the room again, but it wouldn't move. Its doors wouldn't close. Finally she left it.

The corridor was mysteriously quiet. There were no doors in it, only strange things hanging on its walls. She walked quickly, her breathing unsteady, panicky, for she felt as if she were on a strange earth, with no things on it she could name, and no people. She almost wished the voice would call to her again out of the air. *Kyreol. Please return.* There were no doors of any kind, anywhere. No moving rooms. She broke into a run.

The walls spread outward again, flung wide to encircle another huge room. She ran straight into it before she realized that nothing she had seen on the river, nothing of Orcrow's or her mother's world, bore the slightest resemblance to anything in this room. It was as though other people, who saw through different eyes, had made the things in it.

She stopped, appalled. The room was full of dream-shapes, enclosed in cases, or placed on pedestals rising like enormous mushrooms from the floor. All she could guess at was what they were not. Not rock, wood, water, feathers, leather, paint. Not circles exactly, not squares, not quite ovals. Some glowed with colors that made no sense to her eyes. Some appeared to be in movement, though when she looked straight at them, they stilled. Some shapes were huge, weighted to the floor, looming high above her. These had drawings on them, but of nothing she recognized.

Some things had a melted look, as though they had passed too close to fire, or had solidified before they had been finished. These glowed, like stones that glowed eerily at the edge of vision in dark caves.

People, she thought numbly, *who see in a different light.*

She moved among the pedestals as among trees in a strange forest, trying to find something she recognized. Not even an animal's face, not even the stick-figure of a man. Only shapes that might have been faces, in a different world, in a distant dream.

She sat down finally, closing her eyes to block out the bewildering strangeness. She leaned against an enormous wedge that seemed to begin at some point in the air and pour down to the floor in a graceful, frozen moment. It had scrawls all over it, etched into the substance. She could feel them against her cheek like an invisible message. She lifted her fingers, traced them absently, while tears slid down beneath

139

her closed eyes. *Maybe that's what they are,* she thought. *Tear-tracks. Where am I now? I was trying to find the River. Instead, I found this place that doesn't even have a word for itself.* Her hand moved up and down, up and down the spider-weave of lines. The mass had an odd, silken feel to it, like a stone slick with moss. It soothed her; she huddled closer to it, her ear against the message, her fingertips tracing it. Her thoughts melted away, became formless as the scrawling.

She dreamed of running, only not down the confusing corridors of the Dome, but through the black pathways between the stars. An earth hung in the darkness the color of Terje's eyes. A dusty gold. There were no rivers on its surface. But she could hear the singing of water in great caverns and chasms beneath the land. She ran closer. And then she fell, down, down toward the golden eye.

She was carving the message with her fingertip. Her hand was very pale, for she lived among the shadowed caverns. Her eyes saw through night. Her fingernail was pointed and hard as metal. As she wrote, she told herself the story . . .

Water, take this message to the cave where I began, where the blue crystals shine at night . . . All waters lead back to the home-place. Bring these words to the one I must leave behind. I am alone here. I will never find my way back. But the water will take my message, carry my sign to you. This is my place to stop. Soon I will go into darkness. When I wake, I will be drawn to seek the upper light, and I will no longer know my sign. I will no longer know you. I must sleep now. My eyes can no longer see the shining stones. Even they will change. I will leave the birth-water. I will drift in the paths of the dusty wind, and no longer remember you. But now I will remember you. I will write your sign. Again. Again. Again. May your eyes find me when your time comes. When you reach the light. May we meet in the wind.

The water roared, whirling the great message away. Watching it, she gave one cry of love and loneliness and fear of the unknown brightness. Then she slept, and when she woke again she was not alone.

12

"TERJE!" She sat straight up out of her sleep and threw her arms around him, hearing his blood beat, wishing she could crawl into his bones. The room was very dark, except for luminous tubes running above the cases and for odd colors that showed here and there in the shadows. He kissed her cheek and then her mouth, until, in a private darkness, she couldn't find her breath. She pulled away from him, murmuring, then held him tightly again, her eyes against his shoulder. He shifted, sat back on his heels, holding her with his hands. The world seemed simple again, for a moment, just she and Terje exploring something new. She said, or a voice from across the room said, "I don't want you to leave me. Ever."

She could see his flushed face in pale stripes of light from one of the tubes. He was grinning. He kissed her again slowly, and again, discovering all the different ways a mouth could fit against another mouth, until after a while she forgot the terrible sadness of her dream and became interested in what he was doing. Then she remembered where they were.

"Terje," she whispered.

"What?"

"Where is my mother? Where is Orcrow?"

He sighed a little and settled back against the odd writing. She curled up against him, her eyes in the crook of his shoulder, half-closed, so that she couldn't see the strange things around them.

"Orcrow sent you here," he said.

She shook her head bewilderedly. "But he wasn't—"

"We watched you on a screen. He said you might like this room, so he had all the other places guarded."

"I was trying to get back to the River."

"He knew that."

She stirred a little, frowning. "He's a good hunter . . . Terje, what is this room?"

His arms tightened; his voice came against her hair. "He told me. People from many different worlds—in the sky—send things they make to the Dome, as gifts. He said this room is like Arin Thrase's house, full of other people's lives and dreams—" He stopped, as all her muscles froze. "Kyreol—"

"Terje." Her voice wouldn't come; it was barely a whisper. "Terje. I dreamed—I dreamed one of their dreams. I dreamed the message on this—this . . ." She jerked herself out of his hold, turning to touch the writing. She couldn't see it in the dark, but her fingers knew it. The dream ran like water through her thoughts, dimpling, reflecting, hurrying on. "Someone —it's a message to someone. She was turning into something, going away from the water where she was born, up into the air to live. She was saying goodbye to someone she loved. She was so sad. 'May we meet in the wind.' " Her head turned suddenly. "What was that noise?"

"I don't know."

"Someone said something in the dark . . ." She listened, but the shadowy air was still. She eased herself, bone by bone, back against Terje. He was very quiet for a while.

"What are you thinking?"

She felt the rise and fall of his breath. "Just that—worlds aren't so different, even in the sky . . ."

"This one was very different . . . Terje, she used her finger to write in this, as easily as I write in sand. And the world . . . The water is deep under the ground, in great shining passages and caves; that's where she lived."

"In a Riverworld."

"Yes. And above, people live in the air like birds. The winds are always blowing; the air is gold with dust. The water-shape can't live in the air. So people are born in the water underground, and then they—go to sleep, I think, and find themselves living in the air. But they don't remember. They can watch each other change, so they know what happens, but still they forget, when their own time comes. They even forget who they love. That's why the message is so sad. She was remembering, for one last time."

"That's sad."

"Yes."

"Kyreol."

"What?"

"That's a wonderful story."

She sat up indignantly. "It's true! Terje, I wasn't just telling a story—"

144

He was laughing. "I believe you. I think. You may hate the Dome, but you can't say there are no stories here."

She gazed down at him surprisedly. "That's true." A single bar of light fell across his eyes. She watched his hand rise, the shadow of it fall across her vision, felt his fingers at the back of her head, drawing her down toward his own eyes, as gold as the planet she had dreamed of. She fell slowly toward them, remembering the singing of the water. Her face rested against his face; their eyes considered one another, shadow and dust.

"Terje."

"What?"

"What should we do?"

He answered calmly, instantly, "Well, tonight is Moon-Flash. I think we should watch it."

She drew back. He watched her steadily, but his eyes were wary. She moved farther back, and his hand moved again, caught her wrist. She stilled, her own face expressionless.

"How do you know?"

"Your mother told me."

"Well, why? I mean why should we watch it?"

"Why not? The whole world watches it. Even the Dome. I think we should."

"Terje—"

He held her tightly, his hand strong from rowing down half the world. "Kyreol, it's—" He paused, struggling for words. "It doesn't matter. What it is. Did it matter to the man who was dead inside the stone face?"

"Well, he was dead."

"I know, but it must have mattered to the people who carved the Moon-Flash on the stone. They put the Moon-Flash there because it's far away, strange, and it doesn't have anything to do with the living, it just keeps happening over and over—the fire strikes the full moon. It always happens, just like the sun rising. So they found a story for it. They called it a death sign, but I don't think they meant it as a sad sign. It's something that always happens. But it's always mysterious."

She shook her head, bewildered. "Yes, but it's not mysterious. I mean the Moon-Flash isn't. What would happen if those people found out what it really is?"

"Then they'd find something else."

"No, they wouldn't. Because there's nothing mysterious left. These people here have everything explained."

He said simply, "I think everything is mysterious anyway."

She blinked. "Even the Moon-Flash?"

"Especially the Moon-Flash. Kyreol, I don't even know how to make a fire with sticks."

She was silent. She smiled suddenly, feeling a little foolish, then said softly, "It's just that—when my mother explained the Moon-Flash—something happened to me in my heart. She took—she took something away from me. She took the Riverworld. I will never see it again. I stepped outside of its story." She stopped. A tear slid down her face, glittered briefly through the air. Terje sat up quickly, put his arms around her.

"Don't cry," he pleaded.

"Why aren't you sad? It was your world, too."

146

"But it's still there. And this is the world, too."

"Maybe." She was silent, while one of the odd things in a far corner shimmered and subsided again. She felt very tired, as though she had walked for miles, or swam through a river storm. She kissed Terje, wishing she could sit there with him for a long time in the silent, glinting darkness. One last Moon-Flash she would watch, she decided. And then, never again. It would belong to her childhood, like the boat she and Terje had built, like the River itself, with the turtles sleeping on its banks. She would learn about the Dome, about the worlds in the sky. But she would never believe in a story again.

Terje stirred, as though he were reading her thoughts. "Let's go up."

"Where?"

"To the top of the Dome." He helped her to her feet. She touched the great love-message gently before they left. *Good-bye, world where I was born.*

Orcrow was waiting patiently for them in the hall. He smiled when he saw Kyreol, but his eyes were concerned. He led them to the elevator and said to her gently, "Up? Or down."

Her chin tilted. "You didn't give me a choice before."

"You didn't give us a chance. The Dome is not such a terrible place, even though there is no river running through it."

"I know."

"I know you do. I was listening."

She felt her face heat, her eyes grow big. "Orcrow!"

"Well, Kyreol, you were hysterical."

"I was not! I'm only betrothed, not married, and

147

Korre wouldn't want me now, anyway—I know too many strange things." Her words ended in a sigh. Orcrow put one arm around her.

"Hysterical means very upset."

"Oh."

"I didn't want any harm to come to you. That's why I sent Terje to find you. He has a calming effect on people. Even on me." He paused, waiting. She stood very straight, her shoulders squared, her head held proudly, masking all her terror as she prepared to step blindly into the future.

"Up."

The top of the Dome was dark, now. The shielding that protected them from intense light during the day was open to reveal an arch of glittering white crystals. The night sky, the realm through which the moon wandered. It had just risen within the Dome opening; it was perfectly full, so clear Kyreol could see for the first time the scars on its ancient, battered face.

People are on it, she realized suddenly, and tried to imagine them: tiny specks, tinier even than the First Man and the First Woman. Orcrow led them through the gardens, where people stood in the moonlight, sipping drinks and talking softly. Among the trees, directly under the moon, her mother waited.

"Kyreol!" She held Kyreol tightly, as though she were a small child. "I thought I lost you again."

"Terje found me." She paused, wordless questions hovering in her mind. She found words for one finally. "Are you happy here?"

Nara, gazing anxiously into her eyes, seemed to understand the roots of the question. "Sometimes yes.

Sometimes no. But I always know that, when I left the Riverworld, this is the place I was looking for."

"Do you miss it?"

"Everyone in the Dome has places they can never return to. For some, it's their earlier years, for others, a city or a forest, for others, a place in the heart where they loved or were loved. At first I missed Riverworld terribly. Now, not very often, especially when I'm happy. Besides—" She touched Orcrow. "I can always send my messengers out to bring me news."

"I'm going," Terje said, and Kyreol's heart froze.

"You're leaving me," she whispered. She saw him collect his patience visibly.

"Kyreol, don't be stupid."

"But—"

"I'm going with Orcrow. He's going to train me to be a Hunter like him. No one will know I'm there, but I want to go back. Just—" he shrugged a little. "I don't know why. To smell the River, listen to the trees."

"I never want to go back," she said, surprising herself. "It won't be the same. Are you sure you'll remember to return here?"

He was silent a moment. Then he kissed her gently, unabashedly, in front of her mother. There was a sudden stirring around them, a murmuring. Kyreol opened her eyes and saw the fire brush brightly, tenderly, against the face of the moon. *How can they think it's a death sign?* she wondered. *It's a sign of love.* Then she remembered: *It's a ship's fire.* Then another kind of wonder filled her. The people of the Dome sent the ship out for one reason: because the people of the River, not the people of the moon, needed it. All over the world, faces were lifted toward the Moon-Flash: the Dome's gift to all the people it cherished.

"It is a sign of love," she whispered.

"A confused sign," her mother said. "And maybe not very wise. But for now, it's the best we can do."

Kyreol moved closer to Terje, her own face lifted next to his face, and wondered, as he took her hand, how far it was to the end of the stars.